YESTERDAY'S SECRETS

Recently divorced archaeologist Jo Kingston comes home to Cornwall with her daughter Sophie to live with her father. When her old 'flame', Nick Angove, is injured on a dig Jo takes over, but faces fierce resentment from him. Then, intriguingly, human bones are found and the police become involved. Nick is injured, apparently when disobeying orders, but actually in saving Sophie's life. And as the truth emerges, they begin to acknowledge that their former love has never really died.

JANET THOMAS

YESTERDAY'S SECRETS

Complete and Unabridged

LINFORD
Leicester

First published in Great Britain in 2007

First Linford Edition
published 2008

British Library CIP Data

Thomas, Janet, *1936 Oct. 24* –
    Yesterday's secrets.—Large print ed.—
    Linford romance library
    1. Love stories
    2. Large type books
    I. Title
    823.9'2 [F]

ISBN 978–1–84782–417–2

Published by
F. A. Thorpe (Publishing)
Anstey, Leicestershire

Set by Words & Graphics Ltd.
Anstey, Leicestershire
Printed and bound in Great Britain by
T. J. International Ltd., Padstow, Cornwall

This book is printed on acid-free paper

1

A Good Offer

Jo hurried down the tiled hallway and reached the phone on its fourth ring. 'Dad? Oh, great — you'll be able to call in here on your way back. Yes, that's fine. I'll be here, I don't have to pick Sophie up from nursery until three.'

Jo replaced the phone and, catching sight of herself in the hall mirror, ran a hand through her blonde hair. She really needed a haircut.

Her face was even paler than usual from all the recent strain and her clear green eyes had an anxious look.

Whatever was she going to do when the flat was sold? After having had it on the market for so long, she was now facing a dilemma: she had had an offer she couldn't refuse.

They had come here to live because

of Mark's teaching job, which had been fine at first. And he had never minded looking after Sophie while Jo had gone on archaeological digs during part of the long summer holidays.

But it had been two years since the divorce, when she had first put the flat up for sale. Half the proceeds would never buy her anything similar in the south-east now, and house prices were soaring all over the country.

But even more worrying than this was the question of a job. She had been working part-time at the British Museum since she and Mark had separated, on a project which was now finished, and there was nothing else in the pipeline at the moment.

Whatever she did find would have to coincide with school times — and what about the holidays, or sickness? Jo sighed, and moved away from the mirror. There was no point in worrying about that just now.

She had just put the kettle on when the doorbell rang.

In a pair of shapeless cord trousers and a sweater sporting leather patches at the elbows, Professor John Rule looked every inch the archaeologist that he was. In a craggy face, his twinkling blue eyes were edged with fine lines caused by years of squinting against the sun, which had also streaked his mop of grey hair with silver.

'Dad, hi!' Jo stood back to let her father in. 'Didn't you say you were going back home today?'

John kissed her cheek.

'Yes, I am, but something came up, so I'm driving down to Cornwall from here. And having a stop-off and a rest with you for an hour.'

'Lovely,' Jo said, regarding her father with affection.

'Any chance of a cup of tea, then?' He grinned.

'I've already put the kettle on — go through and sit down, I shan't be a minute.'

By the time she had returned, her father was leaning back in a comfortable armchair and puffing away at his beloved pipe. Jo wrinkled her nose and discreetly opened another window.

'I'm glad to see you, actually. I was going to ring you tonight at home, but it's much better to talk face to face.' Jo took a sip of tea and cradled her mug in both hands.

'I've got some great news — the flat's as good as sold.'

Her father's eyebrows rose.

'Really? At last.'

'Yes, I know. And I've had such a good offer that I can't refuse it. The only thing is . . . ' Jo hesitated.

'What?'

'They want to move in right away. They've sold up and are living with her parents, in very cramped circumstances, I gather. So I've got to find somewhere else pretty quick.' She put down her mug.

'Dad, I just don't know what to do for the best. I know you've always said I can come back home and live with you, but I need a job. I've finished those archaeology articles I was writing and the museum work is finished, too. So I'm unemployed, and I can't find anything that will fit in with Sophie's routine.'

Coincidence

As Jo poured out her worries, she noticed, to her surprise and annoyance, that her father was grinning broadly.

'What's so funny?'

John Rule leaned back and puffed reflectively on his pipe.

'This could be the answer to both our problems.'

Jo waited impatiently as he stared into the empty grate and collected his thoughts. She knew from experience that her father would not be hurried.

'The reason I was delayed leaving London,' he said, 'was that I had a phone call to say that the field assistant I had taken on for the new dig has been taken ill — something quite serious, I believe, poor fellow — which has left me in a spot, as we are all set to start work as soon as I get back.'

He paused and met Jo's eyes as her brain raced ahead of her father. Her gaze never left his face as he continued.

'So I was wondering where I can get a qualified field assistant in a hurry — someone whose work I can rely on.' He raised an eyebrow and paused meaningfully. 'Any ideas?'

Jo's heart began to race as all the implications flooded over her.

Her father's was a big house, of course, and she and Sophie could have their own set of rooms. That might be all right. More importantly, though, could she also cope with working for her father as well as going home with him at night?

And what about the other team members — wouldn't they think that the job had landed in her lap just because of who she was?

The whole idea was fraught with potential problems. But given the position she was in right now, what choice did she have?

Jo turned to the plus side of things. Sophie would absolutely love it; that huge garden, the little local school where she would find it easy to make friends. And in the countryside with the sea a mere stone's-throw away, it was an idyllic place for a child to grow up.

She looked up to see her father watching her intently. She grinned rather shakily.

'Oh, Dad, I can hardly believe it.' She took a deep breath. 'Of course I'll do it. And thank you, it's a marvellous offer. In fact, it's a fantastic coincidence, the two things coming together like that.'

He nodded.

'It does seem to solve both our problems rather neatly.'

'It's a real lifeline for me, I can tell you. A home and a job in one fell swoop! Sophie's due to go to proper school in September, as you know, and that was another worry of mine. It all fits!' Jo leaned across and squeezed his hand. 'Oh, Dad, thanks again — I can't tell you what a load that is off my mind!'

'Well, thank you, too; you've helped me out of a jam as well.'

Jo leaned back in her chair.

'Now tell me all the background to the dig. I don't even know where it is.'

John put down his mug and sat forward.

'Well, you know that old quarry that acts as an overflow catchment for the reservoir?'

She nodded.

'We've had such a long hot spell that it's temporarily dried out, and recently a great chunk of it cracked off and fell away. And it's really exciting, Jo.' John's face lit up with enthusiasm. 'There are some very interesting artefacts there, half uncovered by the landslide. As soon as the Cornwall Archaeological Unit heard about it they organised a thorough investigation of the site. And I've been asked to take charge of the dig.'

'So what do you think is there, then? Any ideas?'

'I'll save my ideas,' John replied cautiously, 'until you see the place for yourself, but I think it's going to be big.' He broke off abruptly and glanced at his watch.

'Oh, look at the time — I must be off. It's a long drive to Penzance and I don't want to be too late getting back.' He was on his feet and draining the last of his tea. 'I'll tell you more about the job when you arrive. Phone you in a day or two!'

'Take care, Dad, see you soon.'

Jo closed the door behind her father and leaned against it, grinning, her head spinning with this sudden and unexpected turn of events.

Back Home

'I can hardly believe I'm really here — back home at last!' Jo cradled a mug of coffee in both hands and gazed out of the bay window at the familiar view. The old farmhouse was tucked snugly into the hillside. A small wood of deciduous trees bordered it on three sides and the fourth looked out over agricultural land to the valley below, with a glimpse of Mount's Bay in the distance. It had been Jo's childhood home and she loved it unreservedly.

'It's wonderful to have you both here.' John smiled. 'The house is too big for me, but it's full of memories. It would be an awful wrench to leave it after all these years.' His voice trailed away.

'I know,' Jo said with sympathy. It had been five years since her mother had been killed in a car crash.

'Of course, having Margaret Hampton as a living-in housekeeper helps, but I do get lonely, Jo. It'll be lovely to have you and Sophie around. My own family.' He beamed.

'It's very good of Mrs Hampton to offer to look after Sophie — that will be a weight off my mind while I'm working.'

John smiled.

'She loves children and her own have all grown up and gone now. She's longing for some grandchildren to arrive, I think. Sophie asleep, is she?'

'She must be by now. I'll go and have a peep in a minute.'

Impressed

'Come and have a look at the garden,' her father said, moving towards the door. 'I always like a walk around in the evenings.'

Jo smiled as she followed him outside. Next to his work, her father's second love was his garden, where he spent all his spare time.

'Wow! I'm impressed,' she said as they rounded a corner. At this time of year, the height of summer, it looked magnificent. They were standing on a paved terrace bright with tubs of geraniums, pansies and drifts of trailing petunias.

Below them stretched the neatly

clipped lawn where herbaceous beds and borders carried the eye onward as far as the sycamores and chestnut trees of the natural wood beyond.

'It's lovelier than ever this year,' Jo added as they walked down the steps and sat together under a pergola smothered with honeysuckle.

'You must spend all your free time keeping it going.'

'Well, Margaret looks after everything indoors so well that I can do, you see.'

'She's a gem, isn't she? You were really lucky to get such a good housekeeper.'

Magical

Jo took a deep sniff of the heady scent which drifted on the evening air and felt herself beginning to unwind.

She caught a glimpse of the bay between the trees. A heat haze was gathering over the sea after the warmth of the day and the fairy-tale island of St

Michael's Mount seemed to be floating ethereally on the surface of it, mystic and magical.

Jo marvelled at the beauty that she had taken for granted all her life.

'OK,' she said firmly, 'tell me some more about this job you've got for me. How many are there in the team? No-one I know, I suppose?'

John paused to consider.

'We shall be four men and three women, including you and me. You'll remember Nicholas Angove, of course, but he's the only one you'll know at all.'

Jo's heart plummeted. Oh, yes, she remembered Nick Angove. Only too well.

'Of course. He's still working with you, then, after all these years?'

'Oh, yes, Nick spends most of his holidays on my digs, but as you know, he's a builder by trade and only an amateur archaeologist.'

He flapped a hand above his head to dispel a cloud of hovering midges.

'Clear off! Should have had the old

pipe going — they don't like that. So — the rest of the team. There's Graham — Graham Stone — he's a fully fledged professional. He lives in Hayle with his wife and family.' He ticked off the names on his fingers. 'Two youngsters — Ryan and Lesley. Ryan's at college still, studying history and archaeology, and Lesley's just graduated — they're all local people, as it happens.

'This is Lesley's first job — but I always like to encourage newcomers on the scene.' He shifted his position and looked at his watch.

'Don't let me forget to water the tomatoes before we go in,' he said, glancing towards the vegetable plot where neat rows of lettuces and onions jostled for space between gooseberry bushes, and where the greenhouse stood.

'I don't know how you've got the energy to manage all this,' Jo said, marvelling at her father's stamina.

He chuckled.

'Oh, you can always find time and

energy to do what you love,' he replied. 'Besides, until now I haven't had a great deal else in my life.

'Now where was I? Oh, yes, the youngsters. Well, they have to start somewhere, don't they? And you can't beat practical experience for teaching them that two-thirds of the job is actually just tedious grubbing about in the dirt.'

'But you do tell them the good side, too, don't you?'

'Of course I do. It never loses its fascination, however many unrewarding digs you go on; that real sense of going back in time and seeing what ordinary people did and how they lived their lives.'

'Who's the third woman?' she asked as her father fell silent.

'Oh, Kay — I nearly forgot. She's in charge of finds and also looks after the office work. A very important cog in the wheel. She used to be a lecturer in further education but she had a lot of personal problems and had to give it up. Kay's a nice person, you'll like her.'

'I'm looking forward to meeting them all.'

'Well, you'll do that quite soon, as a matter of fact. I've invited them all round here next Sunday so that we can get to know each other before we start work.'

'Oh, great.' Jo smiled.

'We're going to have a barbecue.' Her father chuckled.

'A barbecue?' Jo echoed with surprise. 'How are you going to manage that? I can't see you slaving over a hot grill and it's Margaret's day off.'

'Don't worry. It was Graham's idea. Apparently he's a dab hand at that sort of thing. All we'll have to do is supply the drinks and socialise!'

* * *

Jo spent most of the Sunday morning helping her father set out the garden. She was upstairs changing as the visitors began to drift in. By the time she came down they had all arrived and were chatting and laughing with her father as he handed round drinks.

'Ah, Jo, there you are. Come and meet everyone.'

The group had all wandered over to the drinks area and Jo found herself the focus of several pairs of eyes. She smiled as her father introduced a huge blond teenager as Ryan Andrews.

Lesley Farmer was tiny and waif-like, with a pixie-cut and large dark eyes, looking frail enough to be blown away by a puff of wind. Hardly suited to rough physical work, Jo thought.

'Don't be misled,' Lesley said with a smile, as if reading Jo's thoughts. 'I'm actually as strong as a horse and as tough as old rope.'

Jo laughed, embarrassed, warming to Lesley already.

Divorced

Kay was older than the others, possibly in her early fifties, tall and slim with upswept grey hair. She had a kindly face, and an air of natural elegance about her. Jo noticed a wedding ring worn on the right as they shook hands. Widowed or divorced then, she deduced, her own experience making her sharply aware of these things. Jo now wore her own ring on the right, too. If it had not been for Sophie, she would have removed it altogether and reverted to her maiden name as well.

'Graham, this is Jo, my daughter and soon-to-be chief assistant.'

'Hello, Jo.' Graham Stone was forty-ish, quietly spoken, bearded and affable.

'And Nick, of course, you know.'

Jo raised her eyes to the familiar, deeply tanned six-foot frame topped with dark brown curly hair and deep-set brown eyes.

'It's been a long time,' Nick said reflectively. 'How old's your little girl?'

'Four, nearly five.'

He nodded slowly.

'Yes, she would be, of course. And you're divorced now, John said.' His glance slid over her hands.

'Yes,' Jo replied. 'That was two years ago. Where are you living now?'

'I'm still in Camborne with the family. Mum relies on me to help out as much as ever.'

That answered her unspoken question: are you married? Not that it mattered anyway. They were nothing to each other now.

For the rest of the afternoon their conversation was general, polite and superficial as they mingled and chatted with the others.

First Day

After the sun had burned off the early morning haze, the next day promised to be fine. Jo slipped on a sleeveless top with her shorts and added dark glasses — it would be glaringly bright working at the quarry in this weather.

But before they left she went outside and on to the patio to open up a large sandbox which her father had given her the previous day.

'Sophie will love this, Dad. It was a brilliant idea.' Jo looked over her shoulder with a smile. 'Oh, here she comes.'

Clad in shorts and T-shirt, Sophie came running down the path, closely followed by Margaret Hampton. Her blonde pony-tail was flying behind her as she ran.

'How about this then, Sophie? See what Grandad's bought for you.'

The child's blue eyes widened and a smile of glee lit up her face. She took a running jump into the sand, pausing just long enough to spare a glance over her shoulder.

'Thank you, Grandad!'

'Oh, there's the phone,' Jo said, getting to her feet. 'I'll go.'

It was Mark, her ex-husband, on the line. They kept in touch because of Sophie, but the divorce had been an amicable one.

Jo looked at her watch and frowned.

It was time she was off and she could see how irritated her father was looking as he paced the ground outside and waited for her.

'Sophie — Daddy's on the phone,' she yelled through the window, and slipped out to explain what was going on.

'I need to speak to Mark about a few things, so you go on, Dad. You mustn't keep the team waiting.'

When she eventually managed to prise the child away and had the phone to herself, she told Mark she would ring him back in the evening, and flew round to the garage to get the car out.

Sophie had returned to the sand and Jo left her with the housekeeper. A motherly figure in a nylon overall and spectacles, her round face was creased into permanent laughter lines and behind the glasses her eyes of forget-me-not blue were soft and kindly.

'I must dash, Margaret. If there's any trouble you've got my mobile number,' Jo said as she started the engine.

'We'll be fine,' Margaret replied with a smile. 'I think I'd better go and get some water and fill that paddling pool.'

'See you later, sweetheart,' Jo called to her daughter's upturned yellow bottom. A small sandy hand was raised in acknowledgement, and Jo set off for the ten-minute drive to the site.

*   *   *

'Ah, Jo, here you are,' her father called out as she pulled up on a roughly gravelled area between a group of Portakabins. 'We were just having a group briefing. I'll run through it quickly again for you.'

Jo looked around with interest as he indicated the huts.

'The big one is the 'finds' hut and where we also keep the maps and records. Kay is in complete charge of that and her daughter sometimes comes in on a voluntary basis to help out if she needs it.' He pointed with his pipe stem to the smaller cabin next to it.

'That's the store where the tools are kept. The canteen is over there together with the basic toilet facilities — very basic,' he added pointing out a couple of Portaloos standing discreetly in a corner.

They were high up here. Jo looked over the sweeping view and took a deep breath of the pure air. There was always a breeze blowing across these exposed hills and she fancied that today it carried a faint tang of the sea on its breath.

The bay, far below, was brilliantly blue this morning, and the castle-crowned Mount was etched against the sky like a cardboard cut-out. The slope of the hillside was dotted with farm-steads and fields, the grazing animals looking like toys from this distance.

'Sorry I'm late,' she said, as she joined the rest of the team. 'I couldn't get my daughter off the phone.'

'I suppose that's the bottom line when you're a working mother,' Nick's voice at her elbow murmured.

'It won't happen again,' Jo snapped back. 'I'm only ten minutes late, anyway. Hardly a major crisis.'

Nick raised an eyebrow as the professor continued with his briefing.

Sympathy

'The site covers an extensive area, as you see,' Jo's father was saying, pointing with a striped marker pole as they all stood at the edge of the quarry.

'Can you see some whitish stones sticking out of the cliff-face about two-thirds of the way down? Nick actually spotted them first. Tell us what they are, Nick,' the professor said jovially.

'They're slabs which appear to have 'post' holes in the middle,' he replied, 'where the central pole would have supported a roof of thatch on a round house.'

'So you think there may have been a settlement here?' Lesley said with excitement.

'That's the theory,' Nick replied. 'Almost certainly Bronze Age. When the quarry was dug out, it would seem that the remains of the village were sliced through. There's another stone on the floor of the quarry where it has fallen.

'I noticed them when I was walking the dog. I've worked with John for so long that it comes as second nature to keep my eyes open,' he said with a laugh.

'Yes, we've been on a good many digs together,' Jo's father added.

They walked around the rim of the quarry until they were standing above where the stones were.

'So the settlement is somewhere underneath here,' Jo said, scanning the rough grass and scrubby bushes of the hillside which was dotted with granite boulders.

'Yes — and, of course, time is of the essence,' her father replied. 'Once the weather changes and the reservoir fills, the quarry will be flooded again.

Naturally, we shall be going into it vertically — exploring each level thoroughly and leaving baulks in between.'

'But Dad,' Jo broke in, 'that way takes for ever! It's far and away quicker to go into it horizontally. Strip off the topsoil mechanically and you can get at it in half the time.'

Unaware that her father's brows had drawn together in a frown, Jo warmed to her theme.

'It used to be the practice to remove every little shred of evidence and reverently place it in museums. But those days are past.

'Nowadays, it's the accepted thing to excavate, observe, record and rebury a site, leaving everything quite untouched. Preservation is paramount.'

As the silence lengthened she glanced over her shoulder. Her father's face was set and grim.

'You young people!' he exploded. 'Always thinking you know better. New fads and fancies come and go all the time, but if it was good enough for Sir Mortimer Wheeler it's good enough for me.'

Nick raised his eyebrows, looking at Jo with what might have been an expression of sympathy or amusement.

'Right, everybody, let's get organised,' the professor said.

Outnumbered

Everyone was dressed in shorts and T-shirts and all wore tough leather boots and thick socks. Even in summer temperatures, protective footwear was essential, especially in unstable conditions like those they were facing here.

John Rule carefully looked them over, then grunted his approval.

'There are plenty of hard hats of all sizes in the store,' he announced. 'Now, the earth mover should be here shortly. He will be lifting the larger chunks of fallen rock out of the way under my supervision. I want some of you to be down on the floor of the quarry as well, to start detailed investigation there, while another group tackles the surface.'

He gestured with the striped marker pole in his hand and narrowed his eyes against the glare of sunlight as he went on speaking.

'There is, of course, scaffolding to be erected before we can really begin work at the top. The rock face where the slip occurred has to be shored up and made safe. The men should be arriving shortly to fix that up.

'I'd like Lesley, Jo and Nick to start on the quarry floor, right? And the rest of you at ground level. Are there any questions?'

'Yes,' Jo said, and her father turned to her, surprised.

'Have you considered using a digital scanner at all to survey the quarry floor? It would do the job in a fraction of the time that it will take us manually.'

Her father frowned.

'I did, but these geophysical aids do have their drawbacks. The main obstacle is high levels of water in the ground. The quarry has been flooded for so many years that deep down it will still be very wet. Anyway, those things are very temperamental — the more sophisticated the technology, the more trouble it is when it breaks down.'

He nodded dismissively at his daughter.

'Now, off you go and get started. If you hit any problems, come and tell me — don't try to solve them by yourself. Similarly, if you find anything interesting, I want to be informed immediately. I think that's all for the moment, so let's go.'

Jo joined the queue for the hard hats and the three collected their tools, before making their way to the former entrance to the site, where the road had once been.

'Well, if we've got to do this the hard way, I suppose the best thing is to try to

cover as much ground as possible first,'
Jo said.

She leaned on a spade and raised a
hand to shade her eyes from the glare.

'Rather than concentrating meticu-
lously on one small area and exhausting
it before going on to the next, I mean.'

'Sounds OK to me,' Lesley replied.

Nick's brows were creased in a frown
line and Jo's heart sank.

'That method's fine if you've got a
big crowd doing it. But with only three
of us it'll take for ever.'

'No, I think Jo's right,' Lesley broke
in. 'Give it a superficial going-over, then
come back and concentrate on the parts
that look really interesting.'

'Oh, trust you women to stick
together,' Nick muttered. 'Well, I can
tell when I'm outnumbered.' He glow-
ered beneath his bushy brows and
stalked away.

A few minutes later, Jo could see that
he had started squaring off the ground
as she had suggested and gave a sigh of
relief.

'Cheer up.' Lesley nudged her. 'He's only jealous.' Jo looked sceptical.

'Why on earth should he be jealous?'

'Because of your father, I think. From what I can gather, Nick's hero-worshipped him since he was a young lad.'

'But — '

'And then along you came. Your father's pride and joy — and fully qualified, mark you, which Nick's not — and you get this post. Added to which, he can't stand to take instructions from a woman. There you have it in a nutshell.' She grinned and adjusted the strap of her safety helmet.

Jo was speechless for a moment.

'Thanks for telling me,' she said when she had recovered. 'It does explain a lot.'

Lesley nodded.

'I'm interested in what makes people tick. Psychology was my second subject at college.' She gave an impish grin and picked up her trowel ready for work. 'I wouldn't let it worry you. He'll get over it.'

Jo followed in her wake, her head a jumble of conflicting thoughts and emotions.

The scaffolders were bolting together the metal bars which, with planks laid across, would make the platform for them to get at the place where the rock had fallen away.

'I wonder what caused the landslip in the first place?'

'Water must have been seeping into it,' Nick replied. 'There might have been a crack in the face for a long time. Decomposing granite absorbs moisture. Then, as it dried out during this heatwave, the whole thing split wide open. I wish I'd seen it — it must have been quite spectacular.' He smiled.

For a moment, Jo wondered why he was talking to her so pleasantly, but with a flash of Lesley's intuition she realised that he was teaching her something. He was obviously more

comfortable when he had the upper
hand.

★　★　★

During their break, when they all sat
outside on the grass in the shade
behind one of the huts, Jo found herself
next to Nick. She had settled herself
comfortably on a grassy mound when
he came out of the hut carrying a bottle
of soft drink and sat down with his back
to the wall, stretching his long legs out
in front of him.

Being of a generous nature and not
wanting to be on bad terms with
anybody, Jo decided to make herself
pleasant to him. She had never been
one to bear a grudge.

'Too hot for coffee, isn't it?' She
smiled, raising her own beaker of
orange juice. Nick smiled back and
nodded, and raised his bottle to his lips.

'You're still with E.T. Williams, are
you? I see it's their digger we've got, so
I put two and two together.'

He glanced at his soil-stained hands and wiped them down the side of his red shorts.

'Oh, yes, they're a good firm to work for. I get four weeks off a year. I take it all at once, in the summer, remember.' Their eyes met and locked for an instant.

'So that you can go on digs. Not much of a holiday!' Jo's flippancy was deliberate. She did not want to go down that path after all this time. Her memories had been buried deep and she had no intention of resurrecting any of them.

Nick ignored the quip.

'Time to get back, I think.'

As he rose to his feet and walked away, Jo felt she was fighting a losing battle, and wondered why she had bothered.

She walked back across the quarry floor, deep in thought, her hands thrust into the pockets of her shorts. Squinting against the sun, she noticed that the builders on the cliff-face ahead of her had almost finished erecting the scaffolding. Their tiny figures in a variety of coloured helmets looked like toys from this distance or like the tiny peel-off sticker people in one of Sophie's books. She paused for a moment, watching them as she adjusted the strap of her own hard hat, and then frowned.

Something was wrong, surely? One of the men had scrambled up from the bottom of the fallen scree to reach a plank that had been dropped from above. He had seized one end and was attempting to pass it back up to the scaffolders, but it was obviously heavy and was swaying about alarmingly as he grasped it in both hands and tried to hold it steady.

Jo, appalled, recognised her father in the same moment that she heard the shout. Then, like watching a film in slow motion, she could only stand helplessly by as he suddenly lost his balance and began to topple backwards. Frozen in horror, Jo watched as her father slipped and slid down the pile of fallen rocks, and lay, unmoving, at the bottom.

2

In Shock

Jo sat in the crowded waiting room of
the Accident and Emergency department.
The immediate past was little more than
a blur — the seemingly endless wait for
the ambulance which had actually taken
little more than ten minutes to reach
that remote spot, and then the long drive
from Penzance to Treliske Hospital in
Truro, with her father barely conscious.

The room was packed with anxious
people like herself, unable to concentrate on anything but their own problems.
A television babbled away to itself in a
corner, largely ignored. It was obvious
from the glazed looks on their faces that
even those whose eyes were directed at
the screen were lost in their own thoughts.

Jo felt a sudden tap on her shoulder
which made her leap in her seat and she

turned around, thinking it would be one of the medical staff.

'Nick!' she exclaimed. 'Thanks for coming.'

He gave her shoulder a reassuring squeeze as he sat down next to her.

'I got here as soon as I could,' he said, 'but the traffic was terrible. No news yet, is there?'

Jo shook her head.

'I'll get us a coffee,' Nick said, and he rose and went towards the machine.

'Here.' He handed her a steaming cup. Jo sipped it and relaxed a little as the warm liquid seeped into her.

'I needed this,' she said, 'but I didn't know it.'

'You're still in shock, that's why,' Nick replied. 'Plus, you never did know what was good for you.'

Good News

Jo raised her eyes to his. Was he thinking about what they had once been to each other — until she had broken away, cut to the quick by his incomprehensible behaviour?

Suddenly a door clattered open and a white-coated woman was calling Jo's name. She leapt to her feet and followed her with a stomach full of butterflies into the room beyond.

The doctor looked up as Jo entered and saw the strain on her face.

'There's no need to worry, Mrs Kingston. I'm pleased to say that your father is going to be fine.'

Jo sank into a chair.

'He has had extensive tests and has been X-rayed for internal damage but he's been extremely lucky and the only damage is a fractured left tibia. A few minor abrasions — cuts and bruises — and very slight concussion.'

'You mean after that dreadful fall — I saw it happen, you know — all he's got is a broken leg?' Jo could hear herself babbling with relief.

The doctor smiled, his eyes kindly in a tired face.

'He must have been wearing a hard hat, was he?'

Jo nodded.

'That's what saved his life.'

Jo thought of her father's relentless insistence on obeying safety rules and nodded solemnly.

'Can I see him?' she asked.

'Certainly, but just for a short while — he's in a fair bit of pain still and won't be able to talk for very long. He's been put on the ward now. Nurse will show you the way.'

Jo thanked him and left the room. Nick was waiting outside the door and she gave him a swift resume of the situation.

'I'll wait for you outside and drive you home,' he offered, and Jo nodded gratefully before following the waiting nurse down the corridor.

★   ★   ★

John was pale and drawn and seemed somehow to have shrunk in on himself, but his eyes lit up at the sight of her.

'Damn nuisance!' he grumbled, motioning to the plaster cast on his leg. 'Jo — I shall be laid up for weeks, and it'll be more like months before I can get back to the site. What are we going to do?'

Jo looked at him severely.

'Think yourself lucky that it was only your leg you broke,' she said. 'I thought when I saw you toppling down over those rocks that you'd fractured your spine at least. You could have had internal injuries, landed on your head, anything . . . ' She trailed off, remembering the horror of the accident.

Her father nodded.

'Yes, I know all that really.' He heaved a sigh. 'But it is so annoying — and disappointing — to be out of things like this.'

Jo patted his hand.

'I know. But you're not to worry about a thing. You'll soon be home again and we'll work something out. You just concentrate on getting better.'

He relaxed on to the pillow and

squeezed her hand in return.

'And now that I'm living at home I shall be able to report back every day and keep you right up to date with the progress — so you won't miss much. And later, when you're on crutches, perhaps you'll be able to come over to the base yourself. It might not be so bad.'

'You're right. You're a good girl, Jo. I'm so thankful that I've got you down here.' He thought for a moment. 'Of course, the obvious thing is for you to take my place while I'm laid up. You are my first assistant, after all. We've invested far too much in the project to give it up now.'

Jo's first reaction was amazement, followed by a frisson of self-doubt. Could she do it? The responsibility was enormous. But what choice did she have?

'All right, then, I'll give it a try and see how it goes.'

★ ★ ★

'I really appreciate you coming to fetch me, Nick. I was wondering how I was going to get home,' Jo said into the silence which seemed to have fallen between them as they walked across the car park.

They were high up here and she took deep breaths of the fresh air blowing in from the distant fields. After the enclosed world of the hospital it was delicious, and added to the relief that her father was going to be all right, she felt her spirits give a little lift. She straightened her shoulders, looked into Nick's face and felt as if she had shed an enormous burden.

'I wasn't thinking straight when I jumped into the ambulance.'

'Of course you weren't,' he replied. 'Besides, I had to see first hand how John was. I've known him for too many years not to be concerned.' He looked down at his feet.

'He was very good to me after my father died, you know. I suppose I've always looked upon him as a kind of

42

substitute since then.'

Jo nodded, her mind skipping back over the years to when they had both been carefree teenagers, always together, always part of the crowd who had whiled away the long summer holidays on the beaches of Hayle and Gwithian and tramped the hills above St Ives.

As they drove the quiet way back through country lanes fringed with drifts of honeysuckle and wild roses, Jo watched the set of Nick's face, in profile now, and knew that he, too, was thinking of the past. The tragedy of his father's death had been the turning point in both their lives.

Fascinating

'Here we are,' Nick said breezily, returning to the present as they drove through the gates of Jo's home, high above Ludgvan village, and Sophie came running out of the front door to meet them.

'Mummy, Mummy, where have you been? Is Grandad better? Is he coming home?'

Jo had phoned Margaret from the hospital with the briefest outline of what had happened. Now, as she hugged the excited child and answered her questions, the housekeeper came following her down the steps and Jo smiled and gave her a thumbs-up sign.

'Do come in, Nick, and have something to eat with us before you drive home.' Jo's invitation was automatic but she realised as she spoke that she was actually loath to let him go. He had been a tower of strength during the crisis and she still felt comforted by his familiar figure.

'Well, thanks,' he replied. 'Now that the panic's over I'm actually quite hungry!'

'So am I,' Jo agreed in surprise, as a savoury aroma came floating out to meet them.

'It's chicken casserole,' Sophie confided as she clung to her mother's hand

and dragged her towards the house.

'But surely it must be your bedtime, young lady, isn't it?' Nick said in mock severity.

'Margaret said I could stay up until Mummy came back,' Sophie replied as she slipped her other hand into his and skipped between them.

'I knew she wouldn't sleep until you did,' the housekeeper added as she brought in the meal and left them to it.

'She's a nice little kid,' Nick remarked after Sophie had at last gone off to bed and he and Jo were drinking coffee.

'Yes,' Jo replied fondly, her eyes on her cup. 'She's definitely the best thing that came out of my marriage.'

'And there's — er — nobody else in your life at the moment?' Nick quirked an eyebrow.

'No, not exactly.' Jo didn't raise her head.

'You don't seem very sure.'

'Oh, there was a chap in Blackheath — where I used to live — we had a bit of a thing going when Mark was being so horrible. Nothing heavy — but to have someone to talk to — it helped. How about you?'

'Not at the moment. Nobody special.' He looked at his watch. 'I must go, Jo. Thanks for the meal.'

'And thank you for your support, Nick. I really am grateful,' she replied as their eyes met. His were grave and serious as they looked down at her.

'My pleasure,' he said lightly. 'I'm so glad John's going to be OK.'

She stood in the doorway for several minutes after she had waved him off, marvelling at the way the youth she had once known had matured into a fascinating and attractive man.

Back To Work

When the team assembled at base the following morning, Jo found to her annoyance that she was full of trepidation. As she clambered out of the Range Rover she could see them sprawled on the grass, waiting for her.

Ryan was sitting very close to Lesley. Graham and Nick were leaning against Graham's car, deep in conversation, and Kay was standing in the office doorway, her face turned towards the sun.

'Hi, Jo, Nick's just been telling us about John,' she called, strolling across to join the group. 'We're all so thankful it wasn't worse.'

'He was incredibly lucky,' Lesley put in. 'He could have been killed — I couldn't sleep last night for thinking about it.' Her face was sombre and Ryan gave her a reassuring pat on the shoulder.

Jo nodded and swallowed down her nervousness.

'I've got something to say to you all, regarding the future of the dig,' she began. 'My father is going to be laid up for quite a while, and he's really anxious that the work should go ahead. So he has asked me to take charge of the project until he's fit to lead it again.'

Jo paused to let this information sink in.

'I hope nobody has any objections,' she went on, almost apologetically. 'It's a big responsibility and I shall need all the back-up I can get!'

There was a background murmur of agreement and no voices raised in dissent, which was what she had been dreading. Jo let out the breath she had been holding in a sigh of relief.

'Right then — to work,' she said briskly, and her eyes happened to meet Nick's. She gave him a sunny smile which soon died a death as she took in the dark, brooding stare that had been on his face for a second, before he looked quickly away from her. What was the matter with him?

She stifled a groan as Lesley's words came back to her — he hated taking orders from a woman, didn't he? And they had been getting on so well last night. She shrugged. Well, there was nothing she could do about it.

'I think in the light of what's

happened we would be better to use the electronic scanner that we mentioned before,' Jo went on. 'It'll speed up the preliminary survey. I'd like Graham to help me walk the site with the hand scanners, while the rest of you carry on down below. When we've got the results printed out, we'll meet up and discuss the next stage. Is that all right?'

A chorus of nods and murmurs seemed to indicate that it was and Jo breathed another sigh of relief.

'If you hit any problems or find anything at all, please report back.'

'Yes, ma'am!' a low voice muttered in her ear as Nick overtook her and strode away in the direction of the quarry.

Jo jumped and her cheeks flamed. Was he trying to be funny? Not being able to see the expression on his face, she had no way of knowing.

* * *

A few days later, Jo entered the office and almost bumped into Kay, who was

49

on her way out.

'How's John getting on, Jo? I thought I might call round and see him on Sunday afternoon.'

'Oh, he'd like that, Kay, he's fretting at being laid up. The doctor says he must rest that leg, but he's worrying over his beloved garden even more than the dig, I think!'

'Well, maybe I can take his mind off it for a while.'

'I'd appreciate a break, too — I can take Sophie to the beach. It's been such lovely weather and we've hardly been out, I've been so busy. Sunday is Margaret's day off, too, so I'll leave Dad in your hands!'

Friendship

'John Rule, what do you think you're doing?'

Kay, approaching up the path to the house, was appalled to see the familiar figure bent over, his weight balanced on one crutch, pulling up a handful of weeds in the border.

He jerked round with a guilty expression on his face and grinned.

'Oh, Kay, hello. I meant to be back indoors before you came,' he said ruefully, 'but I must have got carried away. There's so much that needs to be done.'

'And you're certainly in no fit state to do it,' Kay said firmly. 'Don't you realise that unless you do what the doctor says, you're going to take even longer to recover? You're being a fool, John. Now come and sit down.'

Interfering

Taking him by the elbow, she handed him his other crutch and guided him towards the arbour where he sank down with a sigh on to the bench beneath the rose trellis.

'It's good to see you, Kay,' he said when they were settled. 'I want to

51

know how things are really going at the site — sometimes I think Jo only tells me what she wants me to know. How is she managing? Can she take the responsibility? Are you and the others happy with her being in charge?'

Kay laughed and held up her hand.

'Let's take one thing at a time. Jo's doing well, she knows the job inside out. But,' she paused, 'I guess she's not so used to dealing with people, and she's nervous about giving orders.'

'That's exactly what I was thinking.'

'So, I thought I would give her a little bit of advice, as I've been in that position myself. And coming from an older person she might take it the right way.'

John smiled at her.

'I was going to ask you to do that very thing. Thanks, Kay, I appreciate it.'

'And at the risk of seeming a bossy and interfering old woman, I'm going to make another suggestion — to you this time.'

John raised his eyebrows quizzically and Kay smiled at the anxious look he gave her.

'How would it be if I came round and gave you a hand with all this gardening you're so worried about? I absolutely love gardens and my own little patch is hardly worthy of the name. It would be a joy to me to come and work in this glorious place.' As she turned a bright face up to his, John felt a glow of friendship and thought what a nice person she was.

'Kay, that would be fantastic!' he replied. 'But are you sure you really mean it?'

'Of course I do,' she said and patted his arm. 'Now tell me what there is to do and we'll make arrangements for when I come round next time.'

When Jo returned much later she was surprised to find them both so deep in conversation about plants and the world of gardening that neither of them even noticed her arrival.

An Unexpected Visitor

It was Saturday. Jo was taking a welcome day off to spend some time with her daughter, and was not pleased when the doorbell rang in the middle of their game of Snakes and Ladders.

'Just wait a minute, sweetie, I'll be right back,' she said to Sophie. 'And remember it's your turn to throw.'

Jo sped down the passage and pulled the door open.

'Rachel!' Her face lit up at the sight of her best friend standing on the doorstep. 'How lovely to see you! Come on in.' She put out a hand and tugged her inside as Rachel dropped a kiss on her cheek.

'I stopped by on the way home from work on the off-chance that you'd be in. I'm on mornings this week.'

'I'm so glad you did. It seems ages since I saw you last. Have you lost weight?' Jo looked up at her friend as they entered the living-room. 'Maybe it's just the uniform. I always think those dresses that you nurses wear are very flattering.'

'Well, thanks — I suppose.' Rachel laughed. 'I'll take that as a compliment anyway. Hello, Sophie, what a big girl you're getting.' She gave the child a hug. 'Hey, can I play, too?' She sat down beside Jo where they could chat and play at the same time.

When the game came to an end and Sophie was declared the winner, Jo supplied her with crayons and a colouring book and the child settled down happily in a corner.

'It's great that you called in, Rachel — I'm dying to talk to somebody. Cup of coffee?'

'Mm, lovely. If you've got time, that is.'

'Plenty. You came on the right day.'

Jo returned shortly with a tray and handed Rachel a steaming mug.

'So, what's all this news then?' Rachel leaned back and crossed her legs which were clad in the regulation black tights.

'Well, I told you on the phone about this new dig, didn't I?'

'Yes, isn't that interesting — just over the hill from where we live and nobody had any idea there was anything there!'

'Anyway, when Dad had a get-together to meet the other members of the team — you'll never guess who turned up.' Jo paused and sipped her coffee, watching her friend's reaction over the rim of her mug.

Rachel sat up and stared back at her wide-eyed.

'Not . . . ?'

'Yes. Nick.'

'Gosh, that must have been a shock. What did he say — what did you say?'

'It was a shock all right.' Jo nodded. 'But we didn't say a lot actually. We were in a crowd so it wasn't as bad as it might have been.'

'And you're working with him? How do you get on? Being in charge, I mean — that must be a bit awkward.'

'He is a bit temperamental at times.' Jo shrugged. 'But you know, Nick was so good when Dad had his accident — he came dashing up to the hospital to keep me company, and drove me home afterwards. He was really nice then. It's only at work that he seems so different.'

Rachel looked at her shrewdly.

'Do you think that's because you've been put in charge — over him, I mean?'

Jo nodded ruefully.

'I know he doesn't like taking orders from a woman — he's made that quite clear,' she replied. 'But he surely didn't think that he would be the one to take over, did he?'

Rachel shrugged.

'He has been very close to your father — maybe he thought he'd be the one John would pick.'

Seeing Nick's side for the first time, Jo scowled, uncomfortable. He worshipped her father, he'd made that clear. It would be hard for him to see Jo as anything other than the one who had usurped his rightful place, both on the dig and in John's affections.

'Well, keep me posted,' Rachel said lightly, then gave her friend a sidelong glance. 'How do you feel about him after all this time?'

'Oh, he's nothing to me now — water under the bridge and all that,' Jo replied firmly, and swiftly changed the subject. 'Rachel, I'm sorry — I've been talking about myself so much that I haven't even asked how things are with you.'

'Oh, I haven't any news to equal yours. We're all right. We've got security — people will always need kitchens and Paul's a good salesman. He thinks he might be in line for promotion, too, as someone's retiring, so we've got our fingers crossed. I only wish . . . ' Rachel's eyes lingered on Sophie's bent head and the child's toys strewn around on the floor.

' . . . That you were three rather than two,' Jo gently finished for her. 'You will be, I'm sure of it. And probably when you least expect it to happen.'

Exciting

Jo had gathered the group together to examine the results of the survey. She spread the print-out over the bonnet of the Range Rover and they all hunched over it as she began to point out the details.

'Right, now the data's all been processed it's looking quite exciting.' She fished a pen out of her shirt pocket to use as a pointer. 'See all these round, dark patches there and over here . . . ?'

'Hut circles!' Graham said with excitement in his voice.

'It looks like it, yes.'

'And are the long, straight areas here, and here, perhaps ditches or field walls?' Ryan put in.

'Maybe. But I think we can safely say that this is the remains of a settlement, and a large one at that.' Her eyes shining, Jo went on. 'So now we know where we are, we can really get down to it. I'm getting the JCB to strip off the top layer, then we can start.

'We've got a party of student volunteers coming in on a part-time basis for a few weeks. I'm hoping to give them the pick and shovel work, which will be a big help if this turns out to be as large a site as it seems.'

Terrific Effort

'And what do you reckon this is, Jo?' Nick alone was still scrutinising the plan while the others had turned away and were talking among themselves. 'This large black patch just here?'

'Ah, that I'm not sure about,' she confessed. 'Maybe a rubbish tip? Somehow I don't think it's a building.'

'No, it's certainly not just a larger hut.' His tone was dismissive. 'You can see a black dot in each of the hut circles where the hearth was.'

'That's right. And also, there seem to be a lot of these straight lines leading towards and away from that dark patch. I wondered if they're trackways — sunken ways, you know, made by the constant passing to and fro of cattle on them?'

For a moment Nick's eyes locked with Jo's in an unexpected meeting of minds.

'Or by the sledges they used to carry heavy loads?' he added.

Jo nodded.

'Where do you propose to start — after the topsoil's been lifted, that is?'

Jo tapped her pen on the plan.

'Right here where we're looking now. I think we should find out what that mystery place is, don't you?'

'I do.' He drew his finger across the paper and nodded agreement. 'So we'll be cutting the first evaluation trench along here, then?'

The finger moved back towards the edge of the plan and stopped as he and Jo pored over it together.

'And here, look, is the boundary of the settlement, surely — where there are no more hut circles, just open ground?'

'Yes!' Their eyes met in a flash of shared realisation. 'And that means as well,' Jo added with excitement, 'that we don't need to spend much time investigating the quarry floor, because there won't be anything down there.'

'Right.'

'Which will give us more time to concentrate on the other work. Yippee!'

* * *

By the end of the day the site had been cleared of topsoil to a depth of about nine inches, and with a joint effort from the whole team, had been marked off with tape and pegs into five-metre squares which were indicated by numbers on the overall plan.

'Great!' Jo said with satisfaction. She pushed her helmet to the back of her head with one filthy hand as she surveyed the field. 'Thanks, everyone, that was a terrific effort. And tomorrow the fun begins — when we can start to excavate properly.'

An Interesting Find

With the enthusiastic help of the back-up team of volunteers, they soon managed to get the excavation of several trenches under way.

'Jo, can you spare a minute?' Nick called as Jo was just striding across the site one morning. She stopped in her tracks and waited while he caught her up.

Today he was wearing navy-blue shorts with a very tight T-shirt bearing the logo of an obscure band. Nick caught Jo's glance and laughed.

'It belongs to my brother,' he said. 'I picked up the wrong one. He'll never forgive me if I stretch it, either — it's his favourite.'

He looked a different person when he let down his guard, Jo thought. He seemed younger somehow, more relaxed and certainly more pleasant to be with.

'Which brother's that?' Jo asked. He had two brothers, and two sisters as well.

'The shirt is Robert's, the youngest. He's at university now. The twins are doing Information Technology at Cornwall College, and Jack's in horticulture.'

They fell into step.

'What I was going to say was, one of those students does metal-detecting as a hobby and he asked me if he could use the detector down in the quarry. You know what youngsters are like — he's convinced he's going to find a hoard of buried treasure one day and make his fortune!' Nick's eyes twinkled and Jo couldn't help smiling back. 'So I said I would have to get your permission first.'

'Oh, yes, why not? It can't do any harm, as long as he doesn't get in anyone's way.'

*　*　*

Jo and Nick were just leaving the office hut one morning when they heard a shout and looked across the site to see Graham waving and beckoning.

'Jo, we've found something — over here,' he called.

He and Lesley were standing waist-high in the trench which had been dug to explore the unidentified area on the map.

'Come down and take a look at this.'

They joined him and knelt down to follow his pointing finger.

'Look at this blackened area,' he said, running a handful of soil through his fingers, 'it's extensive — Lesley was working right at the far end and found it's just the same there.'

'Burnt matter? That's interesting.' Jo crouched lower and picked some soil up between finger and thumb.

'There's evidently been charcoal-burning here,' Graham said, 'and on a large scale.'

Nick looked at Graham.

'What do you think? A pottery kiln, perhaps?'

'I did wonder — but there's no sign of a flue, or any pot shards at all — at least, not yet. My gut feeling is to discount pottery. Which leaves . . . '

Graham never finished his sentence, which was interrupted by a shout from Lesley.

'Look what I've found!' She was walking down the trench towards them, her face alight with excitement.

'Look at this!' She opened her hand and in the palm sat a small brownish lump. 'I think it's metal — it's quite heavy for its size.'

Jo carefully rubbed it free of the remaining dirt, and tested it with a thumbnail.

'It's definitely metal.' She turned it over again. 'And it's broken off from a larger object. See this rough edge here?' She scrutinised it, frowning, then at last her face lit up and when she spoke her voice was filled with excitement.

'It's a fragment from an axe-head!' she exclaimed. 'Look where part of the socket has snapped off — maybe through a fault in the casting.'

'Wow!' Nick took it reverently. 'That's quite something. Iron, is it?'

'No,' Jo said, 'I don't think so — it's not corroded like iron would be. I'm sure it's bronze.'

She turned luminous eyes to them.

'So it looks as if we might have a Bronze Age site here!'

'I'm going back to see if there's anything else,' Lesley said with a grin.

Jo slipped the fragment into the plastic bag and fastened it, before laying it in a finds tray on the surface.

'So,' she said thoughtfully, 'supposing I stick my neck out and say that they could have been smelting here?'

'It's likely,' Graham said, thoughtfully stroking his beard. 'Considering this huge burnt area.'

'Plus the fact that there was plenty of tin and copper ore to be had locally,' Nick added. He ran a hand through his hair as his voice quickened with excitement. 'And there were trade routes to the Mediterranean from Mount's Bay down there! They could even have been exporting their axes.'

Jo's eyes widened.

'If that's true, this site could be even more important than we thought. But we mustn't get carried away on the basis of one bit of bronze,' she said cautiously. 'Let's see what else turns up first.'

Agitated

However, there was scant time to dwell on the implications of this momentous discovery, before they heard another shout and turned to see Ryan racing towards them waving his hands in an agitated fashion.

Jo's heart gave a lurch. Not another accident . . .

Ryan slewed to a halt, panting and gasping for breath.

'You'll never guess what we've found in the quarry.' His face was white with shock in spite of his exertion.

'The chap with the metal detector Nick told you about — his mate from college — he picked up a signal and started digging . . . ' He turned away in mid-sentence and the others broke into a run to keep up with him.

Soon they were all scrambling down into the quarry and Ryan indicated an area of soil disturbance at the foot of the cliff wall. Some distance away, the student was still passing the detector over and around a wider area. The young man switched off the machine as they arrived and carefully placed a marker at the spot before joining them.

He approached Jo with something clasped in his hand.

'The detector reacted to this,' he said as he passed her a small object.

With utter bewilderment she glanced down at a small brass button, then looked blankly back at him. Was this what all the fuss was about?

'Then,' Ryan chipped in, 'when he was digging it out the trowel struck something else and he called me. We went into it together — careful, like — and this is what we turned up.'

He moved aside and Jo dropped to one knee beside the newly turned patch. She was looking straight into the empty eye-sockets of a human skull.

3

Out Of Our Depth

Jo took a deep breath as she recovered from the shock and forced the professional in her to take over and assess this latest discovery.

'Right — pass me that trowel, Ryan, please.' Gently, she scraped away a little more soil. As the others watched in fascination, the tip of a couple of toe-bones appeared, then a second foot.

Jo straightened up and dusted off her hands.

'I think we're getting out of our depth here, folks. I don't like the look of it at all. I'm going to report it to the police and get them on to it. What do you think?' She looked up anxiously and met Nick's grave gaze. He nodded in agreement.

'Let's get back to the site,' she said as

they started moving away. 'We'll leave everything here just as it is until someone's had a look at it.'

They all drifted back to the office in Jo's wake and hung around outside chatting among themselves while she made her phone call.

'I got through to somebody at the Penzance station,' she said when she returned. 'We mustn't touch anything until someone's been round to have a look. So as it's nearly lunchtime — ' she glanced at her watch ' — I suggest we take a long break. I'll stay around where I can hear the phone.'

They went their separate ways and Jo ate a sandwich lunch in the office with Kay. When they had exhausted the subject of the body in the reservoir, Kay changed the subject.

'I'll be round to start on the garden this weekend,' she said, tossing an apple core into the bin. 'I phoned John just now and he says he'll tell me what to do when I get there.'

'I'm quite sure he will.' Jo smiled.

'It'll be weeding, I expect. Or perhaps cutting the grass. Seriously, though, Kay, don't let him make you do too much. He can be an awful slave-driver — take it from one who knows!'

Kay laughed.

'I think at my age I can stick up for myself, Jo, but thanks anyway. I'll see you later.' She crumpled her sandwich wrapper and brushed crumbs off her lap. 'I'm just going out to stretch my legs and get a breath of fresh air.'

Jo strolled across to the open doorway and leaned a shoulder against the jamb. Outside, the hill-slope was shimmering in the heat with only a few gently waving grasses indicating slight movement of the air. Her gaze covered the sweep of the bay, the stark silhouette of the ruined engine-house on the skyline and the tranquillity of the valley below.

She noticed Nick sitting on the ground a few yards away, leaning against a lichen-encrusted boulder with a pad and pencil on his knee. He looked to be sketching the view in front of them — or maybe it was the exquisite pink spires of the foxgloves which were flaunting themselves at his feet.

Nick? Drawing? Intrigued, Jo wandered over to him and sat down nearby.

'I didn't know you were an artist, Nick.'

He snorted.

'Hardly,' he replied. 'I just amuse myself.'

'Can I look?' Jo asked, and he shrugged and held out the pad towards her.

'It's not very good,' he said. 'As I say, I only play at it.'

'But it is good!' Jo exclaimed. 'It's fantastic!'

It was a sketch of the bay and the Mount, only roughly drawn, but Nick had captured the ethereal quality of the scene, the fairytale appearance of the castle-crowned hill and the aura of magic about it, as if it were all a beautiful illusion which could vanish

74

with the next puff of wind.

He inclined his head in acknowledgement.

'Well, thank you, ma'am,' he drawled. Jo grinned.

'I meant what I said. Me, I can't draw a straight line — I stick to photography.'

'Another form of art,' he replied. 'You need an eye for it just the same.'

'I love it,' Jo said enthusiastically. 'I never go far without a camera. Photography's such a challenge — even the shots I have to do for work, boring as they sometimes are. And I've got enough photos of Sophie to paper the walls of her bedroom!'

She sat down on the grass and curled her arms around her bent knees.

'Dad likes to have a record of his garden, too, so he can see what he grew where last time and improve on the arrangements.' She glanced at the sketch again. 'You never used to . . . ' Jo bit her lip and broke off. 'Have you ever taken lessons in drawing?'

Nick turned to her. Of course, his eyes weren't as densely brown as they appeared, Jo suddenly recalled — she'd forgotten there were little bits of gold in them which danced when he smiled.

'Me? No. I wander around galleries sometimes and get a few pointers, but like I said, it's only a bit of fun.' He took the book back and pushed it into his rucksack.

'Oh, don't put it away — I'd love to see some more.'

'Sorry, no,' he said gruffly as he began to get up. 'I don't usually show my stuff around.' He stood up, catching Jo off guard by his abrupt departure.

'I must go,' he was saying. 'There's another angle I want to catch while the light is right. See you later.'

An Old Friend

Early that afternoon, two uniformed policemen arrived at the site, and having taken a look at what the archaeologists had found, one immediately telephoned the CID.

'Sorry about all this, but I'm going to have to treat this as a possible crime scene and ask you to postpone the work on your dig until we're sure what we've got,' the detective inspector said as he came striding into the office.

Jo turned towards him. He was tall, with fair, greying hair and penetrating blue eyes, and she acknowledged the familiar figure with a wide smile.

'Andy Farr! I haven't seen you for years.'

John Rule and Andrew Farr had met at school, beginning a friendship which had lasted a lifetime.

'Jo!' They shook hands vigorously. 'I'd no idea you were back in Cornwall. The last thing I heard was that you were married and living in Blackheath.'

'It's a long story,' Jo replied. 'How's Sally and the family?'

'She's fine, and they've all left home to lead their own lives now.' He looked around the room. 'Is your father here?

It's his dig, I suppose?'

'Have a seat while I tell you all about it. Cup of coffee?'

'Lovely.' Andy perched himself on a corner of the desk and listened intently as Jo filled in the background and told him of her father's accident.

'I'm really sorry to hear about John — must give him a call. We've both been so busy that it's ages since I spoke to him.'

'Sure. He'll be so glad that it's you doing the investigation,' Jo replied. She paused.

'I was afraid you were going to say we would have to postpone the work.' She sighed, looking longingly through the window at the perfect summer day outside. 'But of course I understand.' She smiled and looked up at Andy.

'I know you can't have everybody coming and going around the scene of an incident, but I was wondering if I could just have a peek while you're working — I would stay in the background, of course, and not get in the way. If you wouldn't mind, that is.'

He paused and looked thoughtfully back at her.

'Well, OK, I suppose it'll be all right if you stand up on the top and watch from the top of the cliff,' he said at last, pointing through the window at the rim of the quarry. 'But you will tell your team, Jo, that we can't have anyone wandering around down there, won't you?'

'Of course I will. Thanks, Andy. I suppose you've no idea how long this might take?'

Andy shook his head.

'Not at this stage, no. I'll let you know how things go, though. I've got to report back to the Chief Super — he'll have to send a doctor round to certify the death.'

He glanced at Jo's worried expression.

'It's a legal requirement for a criminal investigation.' He reached for the phone, made the call then glanced at his watch.

'Now I really must get on,' he said. 'See you later, Jo.'

Secret Thoughts

Soon the quarry was swarming with officials. As Jo watched from the top through a pair of binoculars borrowed from Graham, she wondered who they all were and why it took so many people to carry out an investigation of this kind.

'Photographers I can understand,' she said, peering through the lenses and talking over her shoulder to Nick who was standing nearby, 'but who's the chap in white on his knees beside the skeleton?'

'I should imagine either the patholo-gist or a forensic archaeologist — '

'Oh, for dating the bones — of course. Do you want to have a look?' Jo passed him the binoculars.

'They're putting up a tent around the area now — we shan't be able to see a lot more from here,' Nick remarked.

'Pity.' Jo was disappointed. 'But those people must be going to search for clues, look — ' She pointed to a group of men and women in protective suits and headgear who had formed a line and were beginning to crawl forward on their hands and knees, painstakingly covering every inch of the ground.

On the way back to the office, Nick and Lesley were walking together, deep in conversation. Lesley, Jo noticed, was holding Nick's sketchbook in her hand and turning the pages as he pointed out something and explained it to her.

Lesley handed back the book and Nick had pushed it into a pocket and turned up a fork in the track before Jo drew level with Lesley and they continued along the way together.

'I'm surprised Nick let you see his drawings,' Jo burst out. 'He wouldn't show them to me when I asked to see them.'

Lesley threw back her head and laughed.

'I'm not surprised,' she replied, her eyes still dancing with mirth. 'They were mostly sketches of you.'

'Of me?' Jo looked at her incredulously.

'Yes. Three or four of them. I guess that either he secretly fancies you or else you're well — not photogenic exactly, but whatever the word is for drawing. They were pretty good, too.

'We were talking about portraits — I paint a bit, and I was asking Nick where the best galleries are. He says I must go to St Ives . . . '

The other girl went on talking, but Jo was lost in a realm of her own, and only the small smile which played at the corners of her mouth hinted at her secret thoughts.

John Is Angry

Jo's next meeting with Nick happened sooner than she had anticipated. She had arrived home, dirty and tired, and was looking forward to a long soak in a scented bath when she answered a knock at the front door and there he was on the step.

'I thought I'd call round and have a word with John,' he said warily, ducking his head beneath the low lintel. 'I hope that's OK. I've been in Penzance, so as I was passing . . . '

'Yes, of course. He's through here.' Jo led the way to the sitting-room where her father was seated in his favourite chair with his plastered leg propped on the footstool.

'Nick! Nice to see you, my boy.' The newspaper John had been reading slid to the floor as he waved his visitor to a chair.

'Stay and join us, Jo,' he commanded. 'With both of you here you can give me more than the sketchy outline of the work which is all I get from my daughter.'

He was smiling, but the look in his eyes made Jo's conscience prick her. She had not given him a full account of their finds at the site for several reasons, one being that the full report on the bronze axe-head had not come back, and she didn't want to look foolish if she had been wrong about it.

So Jo had not mentioned it all, knowing that it would only make her father fuss and fret all the more over not being able to oversee the work himself.

She felt a twinge of guilt because she didn't talk to him more, then was annoyed that she should be made to feel guilty. She had so little spare time, and she had a child she hardly saw, apart from in the evenings.

But on the other hand — she owed him, didn't she? For she and Sophie would never have been here in the first place if it hadn't been for her father. But standing there with both pairs of eyes fixed on her was the last straw.

'Sorry, Dad,' she said firmly, 'I must go and play with Sophie for a while and put her to bed.'

As she supervised Sophie's bathtime,

Jo wished that she had someone whom she could lean on for a change, instead of having to cope with all the demands of both work and home alone. Someone to talk to on her own level, to confide in, to help her bring up this little person who was right now scooping up handfuls of soap bubbles and doing her best to rub them in her mother's hair.

Jo was forced to giggle in spite of herself and retaliated by throwing the contents of a plastic beaker over Sophie's head, to squeals of delight from the little girl.

'Right,' Jo said, seizing a large fluffy towel, 'time to get out now.'

'Oh, Mummy, just five more minutes — please?' the child implored.

'Oh, all right, then — just five minutes and no more.'

'I love you, Mummy,' Sophie said happily, rummaging about for a toy mermaid which had sunk without trace. She retrieved it triumphantly and looked up at Jo with shining eyes. 'So does Ariel,' she added, waving a fishy tail at her.

When Jo reappeared downstairs and entered the sitting-room, it was to find her father on his feet, red in the face with fury, waiting for her.

'And what's all this about an axe-head, young lady? Something as important as that and you weren't going to tell me?'

He waved his stick at her and wobbled dangerously.

'Believe it or not, Dad, I was only thinking of you. I didn't want you to be even more upset that you couldn't be there on site to see to things yourself — or to be disappointed if the whole idea turns out to be totally false. It still has to be verified, you see. I acted from the best of intentions, and if that was wrong then I'm sorry.'

It was too much. To her horror, Jo could feel tears welling up behind her eyes, and she turned sharply and left the room.

She was fiercely scrubbing her face

with a tissue when the door opened again and Nick appeared.

'Jo, I'm sorry about all that.' He placed one warm hand on her shoulder and gave it a little squeeze. His eyes, soft and sympathetic, looked into hers. Suddenly Jo was plunged backwards in time and they were teenagers again, always there for each other, close and completely attuned. She looked away.

'It's OK, I should have told him myself. You couldn't have been expected to know.'

He smiled, his eyes fixed on her face.

'So — no hard feelings?'

'No hard feelings,' Jo replied softly as she opened the door and he went out into the night.

'A Heavenly Spot'

On the following Sunday, Kay kept her promise to come and help John with the garden. She was standing on the miniature bridge which spanned the stream, surveying the old wall which rose high above their heads and hid from view the track through the woods on its other side.

'I do love the way this garden kind of melts into the wild part without showing the join,' she said with a smile. The wall was mossy and full of small ferns and other shade-loving plants, with creeping tendrils of mauve-flowered toad-flax and creamy spires of pennywort flourishing in the cracks as if by design.

In a sunny corner away from the trees John had planted some brilliant nasturtiums which were now as high as the wall and were waving their flame-coloured heads as if in triumph at having scaled it.

A large bush of sweet-scented honey-suckle was running riot nearby and Kay took an appreciative sniff as she followed John up the path.

'Well, I take no credit for that part of it,' he replied. 'That's nature's doing — not mine!' He stumped towards a convenient seat and sank down on to it.

'Time for a break, I think. You've done a really good job with the grass. It's looking so neat now I can't believe how bad it was.'

'I always think that if the lawn is tidy the whole garden looks better — even if the beds are all full of weeds.' Kay laid her straw sun-hat on the bench beside her and lifted her face to the sun. 'I'll have a go at clearing those pansies in a minute.'

'Now please don't do more than you really want to — promise?' John looked down affectionately at her flushed face and grimy hands.

'I promise. What a heavenly spot this is. Perfect for a child to grow up in.' Her eyes followed Sophie's small figure. She was bare-footed and paddling about in the water, which just covered her feet, and chattering away to herself in some imaginary game.

'Yes, she's settled in well.' There was a pause during which they both sat soaking up the sun.

'Have you heard any more news from

the police at all?' John said idly. 'Do they know anything about the chap yet?'

'No. Either they don't know or else they're keeping it to themselves. They certainly haven't told us anything.'

'I wish they'd get on with it and clear out — all this lovely weather going to waste and the work just waiting to be done.'

'They shouldn't be much longer, or so the inspector said the other day. And anyway, fretting about it won't make the time pass any faster.' Kay smiled at his scowling face and as he met her eyes he smiled grudgingly.

'If only this dratted leg would heal up . . . '

'How is it coming along — what do they say about it now?' Kay enquired.

'With a bit of luck I should be out of plaster soon, they tell me. Then it will be a case of physiotherapy . . . '

They stayed where they were for a little while longer, idly chatting and content to be in each other's company.

Exciting News

As the older pair finished their day-dreaming and Kay set off with trowel and basket to deal with weeds, Jo was answering a knock at the door. To her delight and surprise she found Rachel standing on the doorstep. She greeted her friend with a smile and a hug.

'Hi, come on in!'

'I'm on holiday for a couple of weeks from tomorrow so I thought I'd drop in and see how things are with you,' Rachel said as she followed Jo into the lounge. She glanced out of the window.

'Who's that out in the garden with your dad?'

'Oh, that's Kay — one of our team. She offered to help him out because she loves gardening.'

Kay, protected from the sun by a huge floppy straw hat, was on her hands and knees weeding a border of pansies and begonias, while her father was deadheading a rose-bush nearby.

As Jo watched them they suddenly

burst out laughing at some shared joke. Kay raised her head to say something and her hat fell off, revealing her radiant face, and Jo was suddenly aware of how well they seemed to be getting along. She smiled.

'That's why,' she replied, turning towards Rachel, 'you see me sitting around without a guilty conscience for the first time in weeks. Sophie's out there 'helping' as well, which is even better. Kay's very good with her — she likes children.'

'She sounds like a godsend,' Rachel remarked.

'She certainly is,' Jo said, sinking back into her seat, 'and I'm going to make the most of it — it won't last much longer.'

Just as she spoke, the back door flew open and voices were heard coming from the kitchen. Sophie appeared, her face and hands stained red with fruit juice.

'Grandad let me pick some raspberries,' she announced importantly.

'And eat them, too?' Jo suggested fondly.

'How do you know?' Sophie demanded, as Rachel burst out laughing.

'Just go and look at yourself in the mirror,' Jo said and Sophie went scampering off again. 'And wash your hands while you're in the bathroom,' her mother called after her.

John and Kay came in from the garden behind her. After the introductions had been made and Jo had fetched cups of tea for them all, her father lowered himself carefully into his chair and deftly hooked the footstool with his stick.

'Kay and I were talking about this business — you know, the skeleton that was found at the excavation?' He turned enquiringly to Rachel.

'Yes, Jo's told me all about it,' she replied.

'The whole thing is dragging on so long it's getting ridiculous,' he grumbled. 'We must get back to the site soon. You know, I've a good mind to speak to

Andy myself and see if I can worm any details out of him — although I know how cagey the police can be. But he might just possibly tell me something on the quiet — we've known each other long enough, for goodness' sake.'

'Good idea,' Jo said. 'Anything to hurry them up a bit — we've been kicking our heels for over a week now, although he did say they were nearly through.'

'Well, there's no time like the present.' John struggled to his feet. 'I'll see if he's at home.'

The women chatted about generalities for a while, during which time the muffled sound of John's voice engaged in earnest conversation filtered in from the hall.

When he came back, he was wearing a satisfied smile.

'Andy was going to tell you this tomorrow, Jo, before they issue a press release. I've only jumped the gun a bit. But he did ask me to impress on you all to keep it to yourselves until the paper comes out. You will promise, won't you?'

'Of course,' Kay and Rachel said together.

'It turns out that the bones have been there for about fifty years or so. And the chap was a soldier — they've found the remains of a military rifle, also another brass button from his uniform, and most important of all — his identity disc.' He paused dramatically.

'Really?' Jo said. 'So who was he?'

'He was called Michael Laity,' John said. 'That, and his service number, is all we know about him. And fifty years — that would be the time of World War Two. He was most likely involved in some way. But how and why he came to be drowned in a quarry pit is quite another matter.'

'That's the real mystery,' Jo agreed thoughtfully. 'We must get a copy of that paper, Dad.'

'Do you know, while I'm still laid up I might do a bit of research of my own into the case. It fascinates me.'

'Me, too,' Kay agreed. 'I read a lot of detective novels, and this has all the right ingredients for a real mystery story.' She turned to John excitedly.

'Why don't we go to the library and look up back files of old wartime newspapers, see what we can unearth?'

'That would be great!' John looked more animated than Jo had seen him in a long time. 'You don't mind driving me?'

'No problem,' Kay said. 'With only working part-time it will fit in all right. I'm quite looking forward to it.'

Unexpected Hold-up

At last the police had decided that the bones could be removed to the mortuary for further testing. Jo and the archaeological team watched from above as the skeleton was loaded into a van and driven off.

Jo walked back to the base with Andy to collect his car.

'What exactly can you find out from forensic testing, Andy? I guess methods have changed a lot since I was at college.'

'Oh, yes.' Andy nodded. 'It's moving on all the time. You can find marks of, say — old injuries or indications of disease, and clues to the subject's build and strength. Teeth can tell you a lot as well, and — oh, all sorts of things. They can even do facial reconstruction in a lab now, you know?'

'All pretty mind-blowing stuff,' Jo replied.

Andy nodded in agreement.

'I'll give you an 'all-clear' in the morning, hopefully,' he went on. 'We'll just have another close look at our man under the microscope tonight, to make sure.' He went off whistling towards his car.

Jo breathed a sigh of relief and turned for home herself, looking forward to getting back to normal working again.

* * *

Jo was in the office the following morning checking on some dates with Kay, and waiting for the promised 'all-clear' to come through, when she heard her name being called. She jumped to her feet with alacrity, startled at the urgency in the voice, and through the open doorway she saw Nick running at speed towards her.

His hair was dishevelled, excitement was lighting up his face like a beacon, and as Jo ran out to meet him, her mind subconsciously registered that she had never seen him look so animated — or so attractive — as he did at that moment.

'You'll never guess . . . ' he panted ' . . . what's happened now.'

He caught hold of Jo's hand and dragged her back with him towards the quarry. She found she was still gripping it five minutes later as she stood in amazement looking down to where the police team was back at work and surveying a completely new spot.

'I don't believe it!'

Andy came up from below and joined them.

'Sorry you weren't in on this from the start, Jo,' he said, 'but something showed up on the printout I received last night, and we came over here late to check it out — and we found something else.'

His eyes were serious as he met her enquiring gaze.

'I'm afraid you won't be getting back to work as soon as we thought, after all.'

4

Nick's Disappointment

Jo looked in dismay at Andy's serious face.

'What have you found now?'

'A second skeleton,' he replied abruptly. 'Another male.' He ran a hand abstractedly through his dishevelled hair.

'Another one?' Jo's eyes grew rounder and she turned to Nick in astonishment. 'Is this place some kind of cemetery, or what?'

Andy shook his head.

'We've been here most of the night, going over all the same procedures again. I'm satisfied there are no more bodies, but we did find some other objects — a lantern, for one thing, and a penknife — so it will be another few days before we can let you back on the site, I'm afraid.'

She shrugged in resignation as Andy walked away.

'Oh, well, I suppose it can't be helped,' she said to Nick. 'And I am just dying to know what this is all about. What do you think about this second skeleton, though — any ideas?'

'None whatsoever. But they must be connected. It seems too much of a coincidence that two people should each fall into a quarry of that size and land within a few feet of each other.'

He and Jo began to walk back to base together.

'The worst of it is that with all these delays, I've used up the rest of my leave.' He stopped and faced Jo, spreading his hands in frustration. 'I shall have to go back to work, Jo, before we can get on with the dig. After that I shall only be able to come over at weekends or evenings.'

'Oh, Nick, I'm sorry.' Jo regarded him with concern. 'I'll keep you up to speed, but it's not the same, is it?'

'Now I know how John must feel,' Nick grumbled, and he moodily kicked a stone from his path. 'I'll have to come round in the evenings, and you can give us both a progress report together.'

Jo smiled.

'No problem.'

Who Was Michael Laity?

A few days later, Jo was in the kitchen pouring orange juice for Sophie when she looked out of the window to see Kay helping her father out of the car. This was the first attempt by the pair at their background research into the mystery and they had been away most of the day.

'Hello, you two — I didn't expect you back yet,' Jo greeted them. 'Did you have any luck?'

'Not bad at all for a first attempt,' her father replied, easing himself over the doorstep. 'With two of us at it we were able to cover a lot of ground. Let's go and sit down and I'll tell you all about it.'

He stumped through to the living-room followed by Jo and Kay.

'We struck gold almost right away,' Kay said, 'in the wartime editions of the local paper. There was actually an article about Michael Laity, with his name in the headline.'

'Really?' Jo's face lit up.

They settled themselves and the professor placed a sheaf of papers on the low table in front of him.

'Here's what we found out,' he said, reading from the notes. 'He had been home on leave, this chap, and had said goodbye to his family when it was time to go back to his unit. He left them to walk into Penzance to catch his train . . .'

'Of course it was pitch dark because of the wartime blackout,' Kay put in, 'and he never caught the train. His family went searching for him when they heard he hadn't reached his unit. They thought he must have had an accident, fallen down a mine-shaft or something, but it seemed like he'd just vanished into thin air . . . '

'And eventually he was listed as a deserter,' John said. 'Nothing more was ever heard of him from that day to this. Until now — when you dug up his bones.'

'That's tragic,' Jo said. 'I wonder if we'll ever know the full story — and who the other fellow was.' She paused, deep in thought.

'So, what are you two sleuths going to do next?'

'Well, actually, that's not all we found.' Her father pulled out another sheet of paper. 'We looked at an old map of this area, and we discovered that there used to be a place called Laity Farm near here. This is a photocopy of it,' he went on, pointing a finger. 'There, you see? We can't jump to conclusions but chances are that's where Michael's family lived.'

'Well, you can go to the farm and ask, can't you?' Jo said.

'You're not listening, Joanna,' her father said reprovingly. 'There used to be a farm, I said. I asked the librarian about it, but apparently it's a total ruin now — there are only a few scattered stones left to show that it was ever there at all.'

'So we're going to have to think about the next move,' Kay said. 'Goodness, is that the time? I must go, John.' She stifled a yawn and picked up her bag.

'Thank goodness tomorrow's Saturday — I could do with a lie-in. But I'll be round in the afternoon to cut the grass.'

An Old Tale

Jo was out in the garden the following afternoon, playing ball with Sophie, when she heard a voice.

'Hello — is anyone at home?'

An elderly man was approaching down the side of the house, accompanied by a

Border collie on a lead.

'Do excuse me, but I heard your voices and came round when no-one answered the bell,' he said, as Jo took a few steps to meet him. 'My name's Rogers — Walter Rogers.'

Small and bent, he looked like a friendly garden gnome as he held out a hand.

'You're the young lady from up the quarry, aren't you?' His nut-brown face was a mass of lines and wrinkles as he gave her a gap-toothed smile.

'Yes, that's right.' She nodded. 'Jo Kingston. But how do you know that?'

'I go walking the dog a lot around that way and do always have a look over the hill to see how the work's getting on. I wanted to have a word with you, see.'

Jo was puzzled, but smiled politely at the old gentleman.

'Would you like to come and sit down, and meet my father?'

She led the way to the bottom of the garden and introduced the two men,

106

explaining that it was actually John's dig, and all about the accident. Walter joined John on the bench while Jo sat down on the grass beside them and wrapped her arms around her knees. Sophie approached them warily and hovered beside her mother.

'This here's Nan, my handsome dog. She won't hurt you, you can stroke her all you like,' Walter said. Sophie relaxed and put a tentative hand on the dog's silky head.

'Take her for a walk round the garden if you want. Here you are,' he added, handing over the lead.

Sophie took it with glee and carefully set off, talking to the animal as they went.

'I been reading that there paper, too,' Walter said as John folded the newspaper and laid it on the seat beside him. 'Must have been some shock for you to find they skellingtons, weren't it?'

Jo smiled as she caught her father's eye.

'It certainly was,' she replied, wondering why on earth the old man had called on them. Did he just want a chat, and how long did he intend to stay? She had a hundred and one things to do and had promised to take Sophie out later on.

'Only I can remember Michael Laity, you see,' Walter said reflectively.

'You can remember him?' Jo's eyes widened in astonishment. 'Goodness — then I suppose you must be — ' She hesitated.

'I'm in my ninetieth year, my handsome, if that's what you was going to say.' His shrewd blue eyes twinkled down at her as he sat leaning on his walking stick with both hands. The hands were as gnarled and knotted as an old tree and Jo wondered how he had spent his long life.

'Will you tell us anything you can remember, Mr Rogers?' she asked eagerly.

'Walter, my handsome, everyone round here do call me Walter. Well, I knew the Laity family see, when I were a boy.'

'Ah,' John said, 'then you can tell me where the farm was, I expect. I saw a 'Laity Farm' marked on the map, but people say there's nothing left of it now. Is that where they lived?'

'Oh, yes, that's the place. When I were a lad I used to go over to that farm for the haymaking and the harvesting, when they wanted extra hands, see, to earn a bob of two for myself. Michael, he were the eldest son — nice chap, he were.'

Coward

He gazed out over the garden and the open countryside beyond.

'Yes, he loved all this.' He waved an expressive hand. 'Proper countryman, you know — had a respect for all the wild animals and plants and that, knew them all by name.' He paused reflectively. 'He were older'n me and I suppose I looked up to him a bit. All we boys did, he were a natural leader, like.

109

'Then when the war come, he was called up. 'Course, he didn't want to go, he tried to get out of it because farming were a reserved occupation, see, but the powers that be wouldn't have none of it because there was three other sons what could work the farm with their father, so off Michael had to go.'

Jo could visualise it, this sensitive young man, torn up by the roots from the quiet beauty of his home like one of his beloved flowers, to face the horror and bloodshed of World War II.

Apparently deep in the past, Walter had fallen silent for a moment. At last he rasped a hand over his stubbly jaw.

'Then he vanished, see. Disappeared and no-one never knew what happened to him. Like what they put in the paper — the Army classed him a deserter in the end. Nothing else they could do, but the shame of it nearly killed his father.' He glanced at John, who nodded.

'That would be the same as calling

him a coward, of course,' he replied, shifting the position of his stiff leg.

'Yes. Some sad time that were. The family moved away after a bit — left the farm what had been in the family for generations. Couldn't stand the gossip and the pointing fingers, see. So they went. Up country somewhere — Devon, Somerset maybe.' He shook his head. 'Don't know, never saw none of them again. Place was abandoned and just fell down in the end. Sad, sad . . . '

His voice tailed off and he gazed unseeingly out over the garden.

'Beats me how he should have turned up in the quarry, though,' he said after a while. 'Don't have no idea what happened to him, have you?'

Jo shook her head.

'Not yet, but the police are working on it.'

Walter paused again and waved to Sophie as the child's voice called from the other side of the garden for them to watch her and the dog. She had dropped the lead now and was throwing the ball for Nan to chase.

'Some strange things do happen in wartime, though,' Walter remarked, nodding as he looked down at Jo. 'Like for instance, there was a bloke who lived in my house before me. I do live in Cliff Cottage, over the hill from your quarry pit.' He waved a hand in the general direction.

'He were a bit of a recluse like, so they tell me — I didn't know him — but he was picked on and rumours spread about him. Like stirring up trouble, some people do, and they make up all sorts when the times aren't normal, like.'

She nodded.

'I know what a small place is like for gossip. It doesn't take much to set people talking.'

'Yes. I remember there was a family called Dauberman, too,' the old man went on, 'what kept the village shop one time, and they was as British as anybody. But just because of their name, some busy-body started pointing

112

the finger and whispering, and before they knew what was happening there was some tale whipped up about them. Made their lives a misery until in the end they was hounded out, too.' He sighed.

A bark from Nan brought Walter back to the present.

'Time to go, is it, old girl?' he asked fondly, stroking her nose. The dog laid her head on his knee and whined.

'She must be good company for you,' John remarked. 'Do you live alone?'

'Oh, yes,' Walter replied cheerfully. 'I've got a niece over to Ludgvan who do keep an eye on me, but I'm not so decrepit yet that I can't do for myself — after a lifetime at sea you do learn to be a bit handy, you know?'

'Oh, you were a sailor then?' Jo said. That explained the weather-beaten features and the gnarled old hands.

'Spent my life in the Merchant Navy, man and boy. Can't beat it,' he replied.

'That's what kept you so fit, I'm sure,' John said.

'That and the walking,' Walter agreed. 'We do walk a fair old distance, Nan and I. Must be going now though.'

Sophie shyly handed the dog's lead up to him.

'Thank you, my handsome. You can come and play with Nan over to my place any time you like — if your mummy do let you, that is.' Walter turned to walk back up the garden.

'Yes, please,' Sophie said. 'I can, can't I, Mummy?'

'We'll see,' Jo said, smiling.

Walter nodded a farewell to John, who shook his hand warmly.

'Thanks very much for coming, Walter. Call round any time you like.'

Jo agreed warmly.

'Yes, it's been really interesting talking to you, Walter. Thank you for what you told us.'

'You're welcome, my handsome. Let me know when you find out some more, will you? I'd dearly like to know the end of the story.'

'Of course we will.' Jo rose to her feet to see him out.

Walter waved goodbye as he rounded the corner of the house.

A Real Mystery

'What a nice old chap,' Jo remarked, as she returned.

'Yes, he's quite a character,' her father said. 'I had the impression that he's glad to have an excuse for a chat.' He glanced over his shoulder at Jo. 'Will you take Sophie over to see him, or were you just being polite?'

'I expect I shall have to,' she replied. 'I can't imagine her not wanting to play with Nan again.'

'What he said was interesting,' John said thoughtfully, 'but it doesn't really tell us a lot more, does it?'

Jo shrugged.

'What we need to find out now is who the other chap was. That's the real mystery.'

'Yes. I suppose we'd better tell Andy about Walter, though, and what he said. Do you want to do that, or shall I? And we must let the police know about our findings — Kay's and mine — as well, of course.'

'Oh, definitely. You can do all that. And I suppose they might want to interview Walter for themselves.'

'I think I'll go and phone Andy now.' John reached for his stick and pulled himself upright.

Fantastic News

Jo spent some time finishing her interrupted game with Sophie and picking up the scattered toys. Then, as she entered the house, she heard her father calling her and found him in the hall.

'Jo, just listen to this! The phone rang just as I was about to pick it up. And it was the National Institute of Archaeology on the line. Your finds have been verified — they are really interested in the site, and they're sending down someone of their own to see us!'

'Wow! That's fantastic news, Dad. When is he or she coming?'

'It's a chap. Can't remember the name they said. Next Monday week, apparently.'

'Oh, great. It's a pity you won't be there, but I'll make sure he comes back here afterwards to meet you.'

John smiled, a little wistfully.

'Yes, you do that. I know what a grand job you're doing, Jo, and I couldn't have managed without you, but after all, it is still my dig.'

Jo patted his hand consolingly.

'Of course it is, and I shall tell him so, don't worry.'

⋆   ⋆   ⋆

'I managed to get through to Andy eventually,' John remarked to Jo the next day, as they sat over the remains of a meal.

'You told him all about your findings, then.'

'I did, and he's going to see if they can trace any relations or descendants of Michael Laity.' John laid down his knife and fork and wiped his mouth with a napkin. 'If they can, then they'll be able to do a DNA test to prove that it really is him.'

'Great.' Jo paused for thought, her chin in her hands and her elbows on the table. 'Well, if he had three brothers, as Walter said, I should think the chances are pretty good. If they're not still alive themselves, it's more than likely that some of them would have had children.'

'That's what I thought,' John agreed, feeling in a pocket for his pipe. 'How sad that Michael never lived to have a family of his own.'

Jo nodded thoughtfully.

'Yes. You hear so often about the young men who 'gave their lives for their country' it's almost become a cliché. But something like this really brings it home.'

She gazed through the window at her carefree small daughter playing in the garden and her eyes were solemn.

Paradise

The following Sunday, Nick called round on one of his visits to see John and they sat in the garden, making the most of the glorious weather.

Jo and her father between them told him all about their meeting with Walter Rogers, and filled him in on the information that the old man had given them.

'He invited Jo and Sophie to go over and call on him any time,' John said. 'He seemed quite taken with them. And Sophie's wild about his dog.' He nodded towards the little girl who had taken off her shoes and socks and was paddling in the stream.

'He sounds an interesting old chap,' Nick said, as he sprawled full-length on the lawn, squinting up against the sun.

'Actually I thought of taking her over there this afternoon,' Jo said, 'but I'm not too keen on the idea of going on my own.'

'Well,' Nick said hesitantly, 'how would it be if I came with you? I'd like to meet Walter. If that's OK with you . . . ' He rolled over and grinned up at Jo, his teeth flashing very white against his tanned face. She wondered how different her life might have been if things had not gone so wrong between them.

'Oh — yes, yes, of course. I'd be glad of your company,' she replied, smiling bashfully to herself at the understatement.

★   ★   ★

So, a little later, the three of them were making their way across the moor towards the remote cottage that Walter had pointed out on their first meeting. Great granite boulders covered with brilliant orange lichen thrust their way

120

up through the springy turf and the track was forced to thread its twisting way around them.

'Isn't the heather a fantastic colour?' Jo remarked. 'With the sea behind, it's absolutely lovely.'

'It's no wonder that people come from miles away to spend their holidays down here,' Nick said, his eyes on the sparkling water. 'It must seem like paradise after city life. Just look at how many different shades of blue there are out there.'

Jo guessed he was studying the scene with an artist's eye.

'And that turquoise tint in the shallows close to the shore, you see?' He pointed then looked intently at Jo.

'That's exactly the colour of your eyes.' He held her gaze for a moment as Jo's heart lurched, then settled like a stone again.

He's seeing me as a painting, that's all, she thought with a sigh.

'Oh, come on, Mummy, I've been waiting for you for ages!' Sophie called.

Jo pulled herself together and she and Nick began to follow the excited child as she went bounding on in front.

Cliff Cottage, appropriately named, was perched up on a rocky crag facing the sea, its only shelter from the four winds a huddle of twisted conifer trees honed into spectral shapes by the howling gales of winter.

Today, however, the only movement of the air was a balmy breeze which brought the tang of salt and seaweed with its breath and the only sound the quiet lapping of water far below. Floating up from the abyss came the plaintive cry of wheeling seabirds.

Nan's excited barking would have told Walter of their approach some time before Nick opened the wooden gate. The dog and child greeted each other ecstatically as Jo and Nick walked up the path to where the old man sat on a bench outside the front door, smoking his pipe in the sun.

'Well, well.' He smiled and moved along to make room for them to join him. 'Nice to see you and the little maid again, my dear, and your young man, too.'

Jo choked.

Nick, his eyes dancing with amusement, flashed her a quick glance to gauge her reaction before introducing himself, and by the time Jo had regained her composure he and Walter were chatting like old friends. Walter turned to include Jo, with an impish grin on his lined face.

'Nick is a colleague of mine,' she said emphatically. 'He was interested in what you were telling me about the Laitys, so I brought him round with me. I hope you don't mind all of us dropping in unexpectedly like this, but Sophie couldn't wait to see Nan again.'

The old man rose to his feet.

'Delighted you did, my handsome. I don't get many visitors. Come inside and we'll have a cup of tea.'

'Oh, don't go to any trouble,' Jo said as they followed him into the cottage, leaving dog and child to their own games.

'No trouble,' Walter replied. 'I always have a cuppa about this time of day. Come through here.'

He led them into a tiny sitting-room to which an even smaller kitchen was attached, divided from the seating area by a work-top covered with pot-plants. Jo looked around with pleasure. The whole place was as neat as a pin.

'What a lovely home you've got, Walter. You are handy, to look after yourself like you do.'

'Well, I'm blessed with good health, thanks be,' the old man replied, coming forward with a tray. 'When I retired, I took this place so as to be as near the sea as I could, and I shall stay here till they carry me out. Couldn't bear to live nowhere else now.'

'You never married then?' Nick said, taking the mug of tea he offered.

'Never had no time for women.' The old man chuckled. 'Nothing but trouble.'

He glanced slyly at Jo from under bushy eyebrows and she met his stare boldly with a twinkle in her eye, knowing he was teasing.

'Have a biscuit, my handsome,' Walter said, and Jo accepted, her lips twitching.

'An Artist'

She looked around the room which was crowded with knick-knacks and souvenirs from all over the world and decided it was time to change the subject. But Walter forestalled her as he looked with pride around his home.

'Yes,' he said reflectively, 'this place was in a right old state when I moved in — you'd never have recognised it then. Took me nigh on three years to get it done up to what it is now. An old man lived in it before I came — ' Jo and Nick exchanged an amused glance ' — neglected it something terrible, he did. He were an artist, see, had no time for practical things. Place could have fallen down around him while he was messing about with his paints and stuff, so people told me, and he wouldn't have noticed.'

'An artist?' Nick replied with interest. 'Was he well known?'

The old man stroked his bearded chin.

'Now — Charles somebody, I think his name was — Williams? Wilkins?' He frowned. 'No, it's gone from me for a minute, but I'll think of it again some time. I believe he did sell quite a few of his paintings — down to St Ives for the holiday trade, that sort of thing. I never knew him — cottage was empty when I came here.'

At that moment Nan came bounding into the room, pulling Sophie behind her. The child had hold of the dog's collar but was no match for the determined animal.

'Oh, Nan,' she wailed, 'come on out and play ball with me again.'

Walter chuckled.

'She heard the biscuit tin rattle, my handsome. There's no stopping she when there's biscuits going. Sit!' he commanded, and the dog obediently sat down on her haunches.

'Now, maid, you balance this here biscuit on her nose.' He handed a biscuit to the wide-eyed child.

'Wait!' he said to the dog, who sat quivering in expectation. 'Right!'

At the signal, Nan tossed the biscuit into the air, caught it neatly in her jaws and proceeded to munch it contentedly, with a look on her face that was almost a smile.

'Ooh!' Sophie squealed, jumping up and down. 'Isn't she clever! Can I do that, please?'

'Just one more,' Walter said with a smile, 'and here's one for you as well. How about balancing it on your nose first?'

Sophie giggled as she took it and shook her head, then the two of them went back to their games outside.

A few minutes later Jo noticed that the old man's eyes were beginning to droop and he was showing all the signs of nodding off, so she nudged Nick's arm and they rose to leave.

'Thank you very much, Walter,' she said, 'for the tea and the chat. We'd better be going now.'

'Wallace,' he said as he came to with a start.

'Pardon?'

'Charles Wallace — that's what he was called, the artist fellow. I knew I'd remember before long.' Walter nodded with satisfaction.

'Oh, yes,' Jo said. 'I've never actually heard of him, have you, Nick?'

He shook his head.

'Can't say that I have, no. But I'll recognise it now if I come across any of his work.'

'We must be going,' Jo said. 'Thanks again, Walter. It's been lovely talking to you.'

'You're welcome, my handsome,' he said, rousing himself to show them to the door. 'Thank you for coming — and call round again any time. You and your young man will always be welcome.' He grinned at Jo.

'Goodbye, Walter,' she said, grinning back.

'Yes, 'bye for the time, Walter,' Nick said.

'Cheerio, my boy — and you make sure you take good care of that young lady of yours, mind.'

As they collected Sophie and went through the gate he waved and they saw him go back towards the house, chuckling softly to himself.

There was an awkward silence between the two as they returned along the track while Sophie went skipping on ahead, singing to herself. Dusk was falling and a couple of fishing boats were putting out to sea, their riding lights rising and

129

falling with the swell.

Jo stepped up on to a large boulder and shaded her eyes against the setting sun which was staining the sky with streaks of flame and apricot.

'Isn't it beautiful?' she said softly to Nick.

'It certainly is,' he replied, meeting her eyes.

Consequently she was not looking where she put her feet, and stumbled badly as she stepped down from the rock.

'Ouch!' she exclaimed, rubbing her ankle as Nick grasped her elbow for support.

'All right?' he enquired with concern.

Jo grimaced.

'Just twisted it a bit,' she replied. 'I'll be OK in a minute.'

'Lean your weight on me,' Nick said, and suddenly he had slipped a strong arm around her waist and Jo felt herself being half-carried along. Her head was on a level with his chest and she had to force herself not to lay her head upon it and return his warm clasp.

'How is it now?' he asked, pausing. 'Try to stand and see if it'll take your weight.' He loosened his arm and put a hand under her elbow instead.

'Oh, much better, thanks — look.' She took a few steps, then Nick had to release her arm as they came to a narrow part of the track which forced them to walk in single file.

The sun was sinking into the sea now and bathing the water with a shimmering golden glow, a magical pathway leading out to the horizon and seeming to go on for ever, far out of their sight.

5

Thrill

The team had been back at work on the dig for just over a week. They were digging around the hut circles to excavate any remaining walls of the ancient village.

Evidence of how the people had lived their daily lives was constantly being turned up. Apart from fragments of sturdy pots, decorated with designs made by pressing reeds and grasses into the wet clay, there were a number of flint knives and scrapers.

'Of course, there's no native flint in Cornwall, so these prove that there was trading going on,' Graham remarked, picking up a cutting tool and holding it out to Jo.

'These people were no fools, you know. Flint-knapping is a real skill. Feel how sharp that edge is — they must have known precisely what they were doing to get it as fine as that.' He looked up as Lesley called across to them.

'Look — we've found a pit full of shells like these,' she said, as she came striding through the settlement towards them. 'See — limpets and mussels, cockles, too. The tribe must have collected them from the estuary down there.'

'So all in all they must have lived pretty well,' Jo put in. 'What with keeping cattle and sheep and growing grain as well, they would have had quite a varied diet.'

They grinned at each other, understanding the shared thrill of piecing together these long-ago lives through each small discovery.

Jo and Graham had been working for over an hour, painstakingly sifting through the loose soil, when suddenly Jo's trowel struck something hard. Thinking it was yet another stone, she wearily lifted it out, then her heart jumped.

'Graham, look at this!'

He dropped his tools and knelt beside her as Jo seized a brush and cleaned the loose earth from the object in her hand.

'Another axe-head!' he exclaimed, taking it carefully and weighing it in one hand. 'And look — this one is damaged as well — there's a deep crack where the metal's been split in some way. I wonder . . . ' He sat back on his knees and thoughtfully stroked his beard.

'You wonder what?' Jo asked.

'I wonder whether this could be part of a cache of faulty axe-heads which had been deliberately set aside for recasting. If so, we're on to something really big here.'

'Well, there's only one way to find out — see if we can dig up some more! Come on — back to work!'

And by the end of the day they had found a dozen axe-heads, all flawed in some way, which seemed to prove that Graham's hunch had been correct.

Tragedy

'I've just had a phone call from Andy,' John said, coming into the kitchen later in the day. 'Oh, yes?' Jo switched off the iron as the kettle boiled and filled two steaming mugs.

'He's coming over in a minute. And he sounded quite excited — hinting that they've found some sort of lead.' He sank heavily into a wooden chair and leaned his elbows on the tabletop. Jo was just about to join him when the doorbell rang.

'That's probably Andy now — I'll go,' she said as her father prepared to heave himself up.

'Oh, great, I smell coffee!' The burly detective grinned as he came in and laid a document case full of papers on the table.

'You policemen certainly know how

to time your visits.' Jo laughed as she reached for another mug.

'Thanks a lot, Jo,' Andy said as he took a swallow and sighed with pleasure. 'That's the first coffee I've had today, we've been so busy. OK, check this out.' He pulled out a sheaf of papers.

'Great news — we've managed to trace Michael Laity's sister.'

'Really?' Jo and her father exclaimed together, then laughed.

'Yes. His youngest sister, Patricia. She lives in Dorset and was so relieved to hear what had happened to her brother after all these years, she was in tears most of the time we were talking to her. It brought it all back, you see. Of course, she offered to help us out in any way she could, and she gave us a specimen of DNA, which turns out to be a positive match.'

'Fantastic!' Jo said. 'So it's proven beyond doubt then?'

'It certainly is.' Andy carefully filed away the papers. 'That's half the mystery solved, but we still have no lead on the second man as yet.' He took a gulp of his coffee and reached for another bunch of papers.

'Now, I've got something here to show you,' he said, 'but it's strictly unofficial — I'm not supposed to divulge evidence while the case is still being investigated — but I guess I can trust you two.'

'Of course,' John said. 'I should think so, after all the years we've known each other. For most of our lives, in fact.' He grinned and clapped Andy on the shoulder.

Andy nodded in agreement.

'Well, this is the report from the path lab,' he went on, and Jo's eyes widened. 'The evidence all points to the fact that the two men had been having a fight.'

'A fight?' It was John's turn to raise his eyebrows in surprise.

'That's right. Michael Laity had been stabbed in the neck, as they could detect grazes on his collar-bone.' Andy followed the relevant paragraph with a finger. 'And the unknown man's jaw had been battered as if with a rifle butt. He had also lost several teeth.' He looked up from the page. 'The final verdict of the experts is that during the struggle, both men toppled into the water and died from drowning.'

'What a tragedy,' Jo said. 'And yet isn't it amazing how they can find all this out after so many years?'

'Oh, yes, it's a skill all right, all this painstaking attention to detail,' Andy replied. 'Wouldn't do for me — I like to see quicker results for my efforts.'

Chance Encounter

John had been looking over the policeman's shoulder and now pointed to the page beneath his hand.

'What are those illustrations all about?' he asked, squinting sideways to take a closer look.

'These?' Andy shifted his position. 'They're photos and diagrams of the weapons, and also of that lantern which was found near the bones. It's interesting, that — it's one of those types with a moveable shutter.'

The other two looked at him blankly and Andy leaned closer to explain.

'Meaning that it could have been used either as an ordinary lamp or for signalling a message,' he said.

Jo was gazing thoughtfully into space.

'I wonder what they were quarrelling about?' she said at last. 'Do you think they knew each other, or was it a chance encounter?'

'Well, they're working on the second skeleton now,' Andy replied, 'so we'll have to wait and see.'

'Have they found out anything at all yet about the mystery man?' John enquired, easing his stiff leg into another position.

'They have found some fragments of leather, I believe,' Andy said, shuffling his papers into order and replacing them in the folder, 'which may have been part of his clothing. They're still with forensics. This is going to be far more difficult — they're saying that they may have to fall back on checking dental records.'

'Oh, dear.' Jo looked downcast. 'That'll take for ever, won't it?'

Andy shrugged.

'That's the way things go in that department,' he replied, and grinned. 'As I said — it wouldn't do for me!'

A Spy

'Signalling lamp?' Nick repeated. They were strolling back from the site and, as Nick had been away at work for a week, Jo was filling him in on the latest developments. He slowed his pace as he turned to stare at her.

'You mean, you think that Michael Laity was a spy? In the pay of the Germans?' His eyes widened and the two of them came to a halt beside a dry-stone wall just above the site base.

'No,' Jo replied impatiently. 'Not

140

him. I meant the other one.' She sat down on the bottom step of the granite stile and turned her face up to the setting sun.

'Oh, of course.' Nick placed one foot on the step beside her and leaned on a knee, his eyes on the shimmering sea. 'I'm jumping to conclusions, but that was only because the lamp was found near the rifle and the other bits. Sure, it could have been either of them. We don't know much at all about the second man, do we?'

'No, there are very few clues to go on.' Jo shaded her eyes with a hand and squinted up at him against the amber light. 'All the military artefacts we did find tied up with Michael Laity, which makes me wonder whether the other man could have been a civilian.'

Nick shrugged.

'In which case,' Jo went on, 'it's far more likely that he would have been the Nazi sympathiser rather than Michael, who was a British soldier.'

'Was there anything at all found with

his bones?' Nick asked, straightening up. 'I've been a bit out of touch since I went back to work.'

Jo thrust her hands in the pockets of her shorts and they began to stroll down the hill together.

'Look at those glorious colours,' she said, breaking off to admire the sunset which was embellishing the sky above the bay with streaks of flame and lemon. 'You couldn't paint anything as lovely as that, could you?'

'I certainly couldn't,' Nick replied wryly.

Jo grinned.

'Anyway, they unearthed a few fragments which must have come from his clothes — a leather jacket or something, Andy said. Those are still with the forensics people. I don't think they've finished the testing yet.'

The great orange ball of the sun was sinking now into a bank of cloud and the sky was darkening. In the grass at their feet, a choir of grasshoppers was tuning up for their nightly concert and the air was so still that as the voices of their colleagues floated up from the camp below, they could distinguish every word.

'Andy mentioned, too,' Jo remarked, 'that they may have to resort to checking the man's dental records to find out who he was. I should think that'll take absolutely ages.'

'Mm,' Nick said abstractedly, his mind obviously elsewhere.

Jo glanced at him. She opened her mouth to continue, but decided against it. They walked on in silence.

Lucky Coincidence

When Jo arrived at the site on the appointed day to meet the visiting archaeologist, he was already there and was talking to Kay in the office. His back was towards her as he leaned on the worktop studying some diagrams, and all she could see of him was broad shoulders in a white shirt and the back of a head of smooth black hair. When he turned, however, a huge smile spread across Jo's face.

'Russell!' she exclaimed. 'I'd no idea it was going to be you!'

'Jo!' He was obviously as amazed as she was.

Jo had forgotten how huge Russell Taylor was until he stood up and towered over her. He immediately enveloped her in a vast bear-hug.

Everything about him was big — his booming voice, his expansive gestures, his strong arms which were now lifting her off her feet and effortlessly twirling her around.

Safely on her feet again, Jo turned to Kay with a breathless laugh.

'What a coincidence,' she said. 'Russ and I were at college together. Russell, this is Kay, who keeps tabs on everything for us.'

'We've already introduced ourselves,' he replied with a grin.

'I can't get over this,' Jo said, marvelling. 'You must have done pretty well for yourself if you're working for the Institute.'

'Can't grumble,' he replied modestly. 'You, too, unearthing something as fascinating as this site.'

'It's my father's doing actually — I had to take over after he broke his leg. He's itching to meet you and I said I'd bring you over later on.'

'Great. Now come and show me around.' He took her arm companionably and tucked it through his as they left the office together.

'Let me introduce you to the others,' Jo said. 'We're all here except one. Nick works on a building site during the day and comes up here when he can. We've only just been allowed back to work after we had to call the police in . . . ' She filled him in on the story as they walked.

The visitor spent the day touring the site and examining records and finds, including the place on the chart where Nick had first pointed out the large, unidentified circular hump which they had just recently begun to excavate.

'I have a hunch that it'll turn out to be a 'round' or 'castle',' Russell said thoughtfully. 'It could well have been a meeting place where traders would come and barter their goods for the axes and other artefacts which were being made here.'

She nodded as he warmed to his theme.

An Important Community

'It's generally thought that the scattered families or tribal units would assemble at these places at intervals throughout the year to carry out any necessary business, and to hold their rites and ceremonies according to the season.' He gestured towards the bay.

'The site's proximity to the sea makes the idea of it being a trading post highly feasible. In which case this would have been a very important community — and probably a rich one, if other tribes were coming from far and near to buy and sell.'

'Isn't it tantalising,' Jo said, 'to know so little and have to guess so much! But hopefully as we progress with the dig we'll turn up some more evidence.'

Russell nodded and looked at his watch.

'I'll put in a preliminary report of today's inspection,' he said, 'then I'll come down again from time to time to see how it's all going.'

'Great,' Jo said as they strolled back to base. 'And now you must come back and meet my father, and have a meal with us before you go.'

'Oh, that would be lovely, thanks. I booked into a bed and breakfast place in Penzance, but I hadn't made any plans at all for this evening.'

*   *   *

The time flew by as they ate and the two men were soon chatting away like old friends.

'It's done Dad so much good to talk to you,' Jo said as Russell was leaving. 'He gets very frustrated at not being able to run things himself.'

'I've enjoyed meeting him,' he replied, 'and it was great to see you again, too. You're doing a great job standing in for your father.'

'Well, thank you.' Jo flushed with pleasure at the compliment as Russell beamed down at her and drew her close for another of his bear-like hugs.

A tall figure approached up the garden path carrying a book under one arm, and stopped dead at the sight of them.

'Oh, Nick,' Jo called out, 'this is Russell, my friend from London, who's been paying us a flying visit. He has to go back now, but he'll be coming down again soon.'

Nick growled something as Russell held out a hand. Then, as Russell dropped a kiss on Jo's cheek before getting into the car and driving away, Nick stood staring after him like a figure carved out of stone.

He thrust the book at Jo.

'Thank your dad for the loan of this, will you?'

Jo watched, bemused, as he stomped off down the drive, leaped into his car and drove off.

Jealousy

A few minutes later, Nick caught himself driving much too fast in a restricted area and had the presence of mind to ease his foot off the pedal before he did some damage, either to himself or somebody else.

With his thoughts miles away he had not noticed where he was going and now found he had driven right through Hayle and was on the coast road approaching the sandy sweep of Gwithian beach. He drew off the main road and took the narrow track which led down to the sands, parked in a lay-by and strode towards the sea.

It was a beautiful evening, but Nick hardly noticed it. He only saw Jo clasped in the arms of her 'friend from London', laughing up happily into his face. Try as he might, he could not rid himself of the image.

He arrived at the bottom of the cliff and sat down on a comfortable flat rock bathed in the pearly glow of the setting sun. As he gazed out to sea, his eyes were fixed on the white-painted light-house at Godrevy, sitting on its round island like an outsize candle on a birthday cake, but inside his head, Nick was forcing himself to face his own personal demons.

At last he admitted to himself that his feelings for Jo were the same as they had always been, and that he was being a fool to try to pretend otherwise.

Up until now, when they had been working together and he had seen her every day, he had subconsciously thought that the attraction he still felt for her was something that he could live with. And as Jo seemed to be indifferent in any case, Nick had decided he could take it or leave it, until he had seen her in the arms of another man.

The ferocity of the jealousy he had felt at that moment had shaken him to the core. This must be the chap from Blackheath that Jo had mentioned ages ago, and he must obviously mean far more to her than she had admitted at the time.

Nick tortured himself with regret that he had not said something to her on the way back from Walter's place. They had been getting on so well that day, and there had been a sort of feeling in the air after the old man's teasing — he could have told her then how he felt.

But reticence had tied knots in his tongue and clamped his mouth shut as usual, for supposing she had not felt the same? Suppose she had laughed in his face? He knew it was the old fear of rejection raising its ugly head again — the fear of being made to look a fool — that he had thought he had conquered years ago by burying it under the macho image he had assumed in adulthood.

Now, however, realising that he had lost Jo for a second time through his own failure to act, he balled his hands into fists and thrust them into his pockets with a scowl.

'Again!' He groaned. 'How could I have been such a fool!'

The first time they had only been teenagers but had always been close, spending their free time together, each aware of the unspoken bond between them. Sometimes they would be part of the crowd, but were equally at ease with each other on a one-to-one basis. Rachel and Paul would make up a foursome occasionally and they would go rambling and climbing among the crags and cairns of the far west of Cornwall.

Nick's eyes darkened as he lost himself in thoughts of the past. They had been staying over one weekend at a youth hostel in a remote spot on the moors, completely out of touch, when the tragedy had happened. Nick gritted his teeth. Even now, the memory of it was enough to make his stomach churn and his throat constrict . . .

He was definitely going to have to talk to Jo and relive those days, explain that his true feelings hadn't changed, however much time had passed, otherwise he would lose her for ever.

Only when he saw a small child pass by, take one look at him and cower closer to its mother, did Nick realise he must have been glowering and muttering aloud to himself.

Feeling more of a fool than ever, he wrenched his pad from his pocket to give himself something to do, and hastily began to sketch the lighthouse.

Celebration

The house was very quiet when Jo returned from work one evening and she wondered where everyone was. She dropped her belongings in the hall and went to investigate, but as she passed the sitting-room door, she heard her father's voice call out.

'Jo — is that you? We're in here.'

With a slight frown, Jo pushed the door open and entered the room. To her surprise, her father was sitting on the settee with Kay beside him.

'Come in, come in, don't hover in the doorway,' her father said, waving an arm. 'Sit yourself down — we've got something to tell you.'

Jo's puzzlement deepened, and she sank into an armchair nearby.

'Have you been doing some more research?' she asked. It was the only thing she could think of that would explain the Cheshire cat grin on his face.

'No, no, it's nothing like that.' John reached behind him and produced a bottle of wine and only then did the penny drop.

Dad and Kay!

'I don't know whether you realise how close Kay and I have become over the past months . . . ' John was saying. 'The fact is, Jo, that we would like to get married some time in the not too distant future.'

'We wanted to sound out your feelings first and clear it with you before we make any preparations,' Kay added.

There was an infinitesimal pause before Jo rose to her feet and embraced them.

'Oh, of course I'm thrilled, and delighted for you both! OK, it's a bit of a surprise, but that's only because I've been so wrapped up in my own affairs that I didn't notice what was going on under my nose. Oh, congratulations — and I wish you all the happiness in the world!'

They all stood and raised their glasses, and Jo acknowledged how thoughtful it had been of them to consider her feelings when they were so wrapped up in their own happiness. And then she noticed something.

'Dad!' she exclaimed. 'You've had

your plaster taken off!'

The leg was still bandaged and he was leaning on a crutch, but moving far more easily and with a definite bend showing at the knee.

'Thought that would surprise you.' He chuckled. 'It had been itching terribly, so Kay made me go in to see if they could do anything about it, and they took the cast off there and then. You'd never believe how light it feels without it. I know I've grumbled about dragging it around for so long, but now it's gone I'm actually missing it!'

He smiled at Kay and their together-ness was so obvious that Jo wondered how she could have been so blind as not to see it before.

More Good News

'Do you remember ages ago I promised Sophie a ride on a train?' Jo remarked to her father over breakfast one Saturday. He poked his head out from behind last week's 'West Briton', and gave a grunt of acknowledgement.

'I thought I might take her into St Ives — it's the prettiest journey in Cornwall, that branch line from St Erth, all around the bay — she'd love it, wouldn't she?'

'Good idea. Today, you mean?'

Jo nodded.

'I haven't given her much of my time lately — we'll go on the beach and she can have a paddle and a splash in the water. We don't go often enough, considering how many beaches there are within reach.' She rose purposefully to her feet. 'I'll go and pack up some things while I'm thinking about it.'

Her father looked up over the top of his spectacles.

'There's a report in here about the finding of the second skeleton. Nothing we don't know already, but I'll leave it open for you to see.'

'Thanks, Dad — I'll look at it later.'

Much later, she thought, as she went to hunt for Sophie's bucket and spade.

But she was interrupted by the sound of the phone.

'Rachel! Hi, how's everything? I haven't heard from you for ages!' Jo was soon deep in conversation with her friend. 'Big news? Oh, yes, I'm dying to hear . . . but today . . . I'll tell you what — I'm taking Sophie out for the day — why don't you come along, too?' She outlined their plans.

'And we can have a good old chat. Great! We'll meet you at the station, then.' Jo put the phone down with a smile.

★　★　★

Sophie's tongue was never still as they boarded the train and set off on their journey.

'Look at all those birds on the water, Mummy, can you see them? They're swimming — like the ducks in the park.'

Jo nodded, looking fondly at her excited little daughter, whose nose was flattened against the glass of the window as the train wound its way out of the station and along beside a stretch of mudflats which was alive with hundreds of waterfowl.

'Yes, and can you see the heron over there?' She pointed to the great bird standing still as a statue on its stilt-like legs. 'He's waiting to catch a fish for his lunch.'

Soon the train had left the nature reserve behind and was following the curving line of the bay, running just above the beach all the way into St Ives, which lay spread out before them, pretty as a picture postcard. The sea was a calm and perfect turquoise blue and Godrevy lighthouse at its farther side gleamed white in the morning sun.

The three of them made straight for the beach and spent a pleasant hour or so building sandcastles and jumping over the waves as they paddled and splashed in the sea.

'A cup of coffee, I think?' Jo turned to Rachel as they were picking up their things. 'If we go back along the harbour we could sit at an outside table in that café overlooking the sand. Sophie will be quite safe down there where we can see her, and we can have a chat.'

The three of them strolled along the crowded harbour front, mingling with the holidaymakers and looking at the shops, cafés, galleries and amusements which lined the street, and were soon comfortably settled in the sun with their drinks. Sophie finished her milk-shake and biscuits long before the adults, and began fidgeting in her seat as her mother had known she would.

'You can go and play on the beach again until we're ready to go, Sophie — stay just below here where I can see you.'

The tide was out and the harbour beach was smooth and enticing, with little pools left by the ebbing water sparkling in the sun. It was a child's paradise and the little girl needed no further encouragement. Jo took her over the road and she was off in a flash of red shorts and scampering brown legs.

'Peace at last!' Jo laughed. 'More coffee?' She held the pot poised over Rachel's cup. 'I'll be mother, shall I?'

Rachel giggled, then drew closer to Jo across the table and dropped her voice.

'And you won't be the only one for much longer.' Her eyes shone with excitement. 'Jo — I'm pregnant — at last!'

Jo grabbed her friend's hand and squeezed it.

'Oh, Rachel, that's fantastic. I suppose Paul's delighted?'

'He's over the moon!'

The two women launched into a long and cosy chat about motherhood which lasted until Sophie came back dishevelled, covered in sand and hungry again.

'Well, we've been here so long that we might as well order lunch now — what do you think?' Jo said with a laugh as she glanced at her watch.

'Fine by me,' Rachel agreed. 'If we

have it early and get it out of the way, that'll give us a nice long afternoon.'

Grave

Much later when they were all replete but too lazy to move, the conversation turned to the past, as they exchanged memories of mutual friends and incidents which they had shared.

'Do you and Nick ever talk about that time — you know ... ' Rachel asked, her eyes on the distant lighthouse which seemed to be almost floating in the turquoise water, a faraway look on her face.

'No. Never.' Jo's face was grave as she shook her head. 'Sometimes I catch him looking at me in a certain way, and I'm sure he's about to say something, but then he'll turn away and stalk off.'

Rachel nodded as their eyes met and Jo absently fiddled with a napkin, tearing it into tiny shreds.

'After the tragedy I'm sure that he

subconsciously blamed me, you see,' she said as she swallowed down the lump in her throat which was threatening to choke her. 'I suppose he had to blame somebody.'

6

Awkward

At the team meeting one morning, Jo was briefing all her colleagues on the work which was still to be done and giving an outline of how they were going to proceed.

'We're making such good progress with the excavation of the huts,' she said, 'that we don't all need to be working there any more. I think we should explore in more detail the burnt area where Lesley found that axe-head the other day. So, Graham, you join me for an in-depth survey over there while Ryan and Lesley carry on with the hut circles. OK?'

Nodding, they moved off to take care of their assigned jobs, and worked absorbedly for a while.

Eventually, Jo rose to her feet and

dusted herself off.

'I need to go back to the office and see if we have anything on prehistoric smelting techniques. It might give us a lead on what we should be looking for here. You carry on in the meantime — I won't be long.'

Graham gave a grunt of assent without looking up from his work.

On her way back, Jo bumped into Nick, who was coming the other way.

'Oh, hi — I didn't expect to see you today,' she said, immediately feeling slightly awkward.

Nick ran a hand through his springy hair and smiled.

'I'm between jobs, so I'm free for a few days. Thought I'd come up and see how things are going.'

Jo filled him in as they strolled back together.

'You can come and help me look out some documentation on ancient smelting,' she said, thrusting a hand into her jeans pocket as she searched for a tissue to wipe her dirty fingers. As she did so something else came with it.

'Oh — I forgot I had this leaflet. There's an exhibition of Charles Wallace paintings over at Newlyn soon.' She handed the crumpled paper to him. 'I thought we might go, if you're interested.'

'Of course I am. Thanks.' Nick studied the information, then glanced enquiringly up at Jo. 'What about today?'

'Depends how it goes,' she replied. 'But maybe this afternoon?'

Nick nodded.

'I'll be around all day. We can decide later.'

Disturbing

By lunchtime Jo had decided to take the plunge and visit the art exhibition that afternoon.

Having arrived in Penzance, they parked the car near the harbour.

'I quite fancy a walk,' Jo said, looking

out over the magnificent sweep of Mount's Bay. 'How about you? Shall we go along the prom into Newlyn?'

'Sure, that's fine by me,' Nick said, and they set off. The pavement thronged with holidaymakers and he caught Jo's hand in his to steer her through a knot of people. She was very conscious of his proximity and also of the hand, but it was only an automatic reaction on his part, wasn't it? It didn't mean anything.

'Oh, look,' Jo said. 'The *Scillonian's* just leaving. Let's watch it, shall we?' She turned and ran on to the quay.

The passenger ship *Scillonian* was just leaving its berth at Penzance on its regular route to the Isles of Scilly, and Nick and Jo stood side by side and watched it getting ever smaller until it looked like a child's toy in the distance.

'I've never been over there by boat, have you?' Nick remarked.

'Not me,' Jo replied. 'I don't fancy it one bit. They say it's a notoriously rough crossing, don't they?' She laughed.

'I'm one of the world's worst sailors — give me the helicopter any day.'

They continued their walk and were approaching Newlyn when Jo glanced up at a large billboard.

'Oh, there's the poster I saw in St Ives. *Paintings by the Newlyn School,*' she read. 'That's what they called the artists who came down here in the Twenties and Thirties, isn't it? They formed their own little group and several of them settled in Cornwall for good.'

'Yes, that's right.' Nick nodded, following her pointing finger. 'Stanhope Forbes and his wife were two of them, and then there was that chap who was known by the name of the place where he lived — 'Lamorna' Birch — I've no idea what his real first name was.'

'Oh, here we are, look.' Jo followed Nick as he turned in at the entrance to the gallery. 'Let's get a catalogue. It's a big exhibition — spread over several rooms, I think.'

'We can leave Charles Wallace till last

— his work seems to be all together, upstairs,' Nick said.

They looked with interest at the paintings lining the walls.

'I recognise that one,' Jo said, pointing. 'You see it on postcards and all sorts of places.'

'Oh, yes.' Nick looked over his shoulder. 'The fishing boats unloading on the beach, you mean.' He came to stand at her elbow. 'That's a Stanhope Forbes. Marvellous detail, isn't it?'

They spent some time examining the different paintings and then they left the Newlyn artists behind, and came across a section of totally different paintings. These were in water-colour and were composed of imaginative and dreamy landscapes full of dark caverns and towering crags. Mist-shrouded peaks loomed over deep valleys full of rushing water and thick, mysterious forests.

The name of the artist leapt out at them in letters ten feet tall.

'Here he is — this is the Charles

Wallace section,' Jo said, leaning closer. In this particular painting, a waterfall was dropping in a silver cascade down to a magical river far below, and a faerie-like couple were drifting in a rose-pink boat beneath a moon the colour of pearl.

It was heart-stoppingly beautiful, remote and haunting. This man was a master of his craft. Jo caught her breath and looked at the next. There were half a dozen in a similar vein, all equally enchanting, but somehow disturbing as well.

Tormented Soul

'Nick,' she said quietly, 'there's something about these that makes my flesh creep. Do you feel it, too?'

'Yeah, a bit.' Nick was peering intently at one of the scenes and was only half listening. He looked up after a moment. 'It's because nothing is quite what it seems. Look closer and you'll see what I mean.'

Jo did as he said and realised that Nick was right. For none of the idyllic scenes was what it seemed at first glance. In each one something dark was about to occur; there was danger in this paradise.

The couple in the boat were heading helplessly towards a foaming weir with a sheer drop on to savage-looking rocks below. In another one, the leafless trees of a serene-looking forest had, on closer inspection, sinister faces concealed in the grain of their bark and were reaching out clawlike 'arms' to ensnare the innocent couple strolling beneath.

Jo shivered and reached for the catalogue in Nick's hand.

'*Charles Wallace*,' she read aloud, '*painted many illustrations in water-colour for books of children's fairy tales* . . . Fairy tales — oh, that's what they are, Nick.'

He glanced at the booklet as Jo went on reading.

' . . . *and is also known for his*

vigorous seascapes in oils of the north Cornish coast which he loved . . . These are over here, look.' She pointed.

They were hanging in an adjoining room, powerful and superbly executed images of the sea in its wilder aspects. There was nothing peaceful or serene here either, Jo noted. Crashing waves hurled themselves on to savage rocks and shattered in a welter of ragged foam. Pitiless black cliffs soared high into space, the sparse vegetation clinging to their crevices scoured by salt spray and lashed by furious gales.

They were as disturbing in their way as the book illustrations had been, and Jo formed the impression of the artist as a tormented soul who was trying to find relief for his own emotions in his portrayal of the harsher side of nature.

'So this is the man who used to live in Walter's cottage,' she said reflectively, as Nick crossed the room to join her. 'They're very impressive, aren't they? That one of Botallack with the mine perched on the cliff, and all the

172

churning water around the rocks below — very atmospheric.'

Nick grunted his agreement.

'Let's sit down and look at this catalogue properly — it gives a potted biography of each artist,' Jo added. 'Besides, my feet are killing me.'

'Right.' Nick flopped down beside her on the leather-covered bench. 'Find the section on Charles Wallace,' he said, looking over her shoulder.

Black Mood

Jo found the page and began to read.

' . . . *born 1915 in England of German parents, Karl Wallach changed his name to Charles Wallace in 1939.*' Jo gasped and her eyes met Nick's. 'Are you thinking what I'm thinking?' she said quietly, and he nodded.

'Go on — what else is there?'

'*His most successful works were illustrations for children's books, mostly fairy tales, where his imaginative style is* seen at its best. Later in life he turned to painting moody and evocative seascapes, and these are very much sought after today. Charles Wallace faded from the public eye in about 1943, when sales of art took a steep dive because of World War Two, and he produced nothing of note after that time . . . '

Jo raised her eyes to Nick's face.

'Interesting,' she said thoughtfully, as she closed the catalogue. 'I think I should go and see Walter again. Don't you?'

As they left the exhibition Jo kept chatting about what they had seen, but on the walk back to the car there were crowds thronging the pavement and for a large amount of the time they were forced to keep to single file. And the density of the traffic leaving Penzance as they drove home meant that Nick was in no position to hold a lengthy conversation. By the time they arrived back he seemed to be in a thoroughly black mood.

'I'll go round and see Walter tomorrow,' Jo said brightly as she opened the car door.

Nick grunted in reply.

Thinking back over the afternoon, Jo racked her brains for a clue to what she might have done to upset him, but her conscience was clear. She'd enjoyed the outing and had had the impression that Nick had done so as well, until now. She shrugged and slammed the door of the car.

'See you tomorrow,' she called and raised a hand. As he roared off down the road she watched until the tail lights of the car had disappeared around a bend, and sighed.

A Good Memory

'Walter, I need your help,' Jo said. She was once more sitting in the old man's spotless kitchen drinking tea, having left Sophie behind this time. John and Kay had already arranged to take her to the park, and she had purposely not told her daughter where she was going. If Sophie had had the slightest inkling that she would be seeing Nan, leaving her behind would have spelled big trouble.

'If I can, my handsome.' Walter's blue eyes regarded her steadily. 'In what way's that then?'

Jo leaned forward in her chair.

'It's about Charles Wallace — the painter who lived here once. Do you know anything at all about him? We saw an exhibition of his work yesterday and we got interested in him as a person. I know you were away at sea a lot and didn't know him yourself, but would there be anyone else around here that might have done?'

'Let's see.' Walter scratched his head. 'Your best bet would be to go down to the village shop in Ludgvan and talk to Bessie. Bessie Phillips. Her and I was at school together — she were a few years younger'n me — but she do still live in the house what she were born in. Her daughter do keep the shop now, though, along with her daughter and her husband.

'There isn't much that do go on what Bessie don't know about, and she've a good memory for the old days. I must go over there again myself soon. We do enjoy a chat every now and then, Bessie and me.'

'Right, Walter, thanks a lot. I could do that before I go home. I brought the car today.' Jo picked up her tea and glanced at the grandfather clock in the corner.

She stayed long enough to be polite, then excused herself and drove to Ludgvan, where the owners lived over the shop and were fortunately at home.

She was ushered into the parlour where an old lady with cheeks like apples and snowy white hair welcomed her.

'Oh, yes, we do go back a long way, Walter and me. Some lad he were when he were young, I can tell you.'

Her eyes twinkled and Jo could see a

shade of the lively girl she must have been then.

'Charles Wallace, you say? Oh, yes, I remember him right enough,' the old lady said in reply to Jo's question. 'Lived over in Falmouth, he did.'

'Falmouth?' Jo's face dropped. It must be the wrong person — or Bessie was confused. But when she looked at the bright eyes regarding her like those of a perky robin, she decided that 'confused' was the last word that applied to her.

'But I thought he lived up on the moors at Cliff Cottage — where Walter lives now, you know?'

'Oh, he never lived there permanently, my handsome. No, Badgers Hill was only his weekend retreat, like. Where he used to come and do his painting. And cycling — a great bicyclist he were. Sometimes he would cycle all the way over from Falmouth, in the summertime.'

'Do you remember anything more about him, Mrs Phillips — was he married? What did he do for a living?'

No Friends

'Call me Bessie, maid, everybody do.' The old lady took off her spectacles and began to polish them. 'No, he weren't never married so far as I know. Quiet fellow he were, kept himself to himself, like — polite enough, but not the chatty sort. Always on his own he were, never seemed to have no friends — leastwise, not down here, that is.' She held the glasses up to the light and gazed through them.

'Used to come in the shop regular for his groceries,' she went on, 'when he was on his way up to the cottage. That's the only reason I knew him at all. Always looked the same, he did. Used to wear a baggy old pullover with great leather patches on the elbows — never saw him in nothing else.' She chuckled as she popped the spectacles back on her nose and peered through them. 'What else was it you said?'

'Do you know what he did for a living?' Jo asked her. 'And whereabouts in Falmouth he lived?'

'Don't know where he lived, but he used to work at the coastguard station. I asked him once, just for something to say when I was wrapping up his bread — I remember it well. He said he was something or other in the office there and how much he loved boats and the sea, especially the north coast. Because it was more rugged than where he lived, and that's why he bought that there cottage. Seen his paintings, have you? A lot of them was of the sea, weren't they?'

Jo nodded.

'He was a very good artist. I went to an exhibition of his work only yesterday. I was really impressed.'

The conversation turned to general matters after that and Jo soon made her farewells. Bessie had given her a lot to think about.

Interested

'Oh, there you are, Jo!' Her father came a few steps down the path to meet her as she returned home. 'I was looking all over for you — I had a phone call from Andy while you were out.'

Leaning on a stick, for he could manage without the crutches now, John accompanied her into the house and subsided into an armchair as Jo stood leaning against the door jamb, waiting to hear the latest news.

'So what did he have to say?' she prompted, as her father took out his pipe.

'Well, you know he told us that they'd traced Michael Laity's sister?'

Jo nodded.

'Well, her name's Patricia.' He tamped tobacco firmly into the bowl. 'And he said that she wants to come down to revisit the district where she lived and see for herself where it all happened.'

John put a match to the tobacco, leaned back in his chair and released a cloud of blue smoke as he took the first puff of the pipe.

'And Andy also asked would we like

to meet her?' He glanced up at Jo.

'Of course we would, wouldn't we?' Jo looked eagerly back at him and he nodded.

'Yes, I'm glad you feel the same way, because I told Andy that after I'd cleared it with you, naturally, perhaps we could invite her to stay with us here over the weekend.'

'Great idea,' Jo replied. 'This coming weekend, you mean?'

John nodded.

'She's arriving on Friday evening, I think. Now that I know you're agreeable, I'll phone Andy back and get the details.'

⋆   ⋆   ⋆

Patricia Stanton was a short, motherly figure with wiry grey hair, a pair of lively blue eyes and a generous smile. Smart in a floral print dress and a navy cardigan, there was a sprightly air about her in spite of her age and she and Jo immediately took to one another, falling into easy conversation with no trace of awkwardness.

They were sitting in the lounge with their coffee after a meal on the evening of Patricia's arrival, when she produced a photograph album from a bag and laid it on the small table in front of her.

'I've brought along some of our family photos to show you,' she said, feeling for her spectacles. 'If you're interested, that is?'

'Of course we are!' Jo and her father said together.

'This page shows us all when we were young and living on the farm.'

Jo and John drew closer and looked over her shoulder.

'There's Michael.'

The End Of Childhood

A tall thin boy of about twelve looked seriously back at them. He was walking a dog on a lead down a country lane, and was half-turned towards the camera, looking back over his shoulder. Even in the grainy black and white picture he showed promise of becoming a handsome man.

Patricia pointed to another snapshot of two children building a sandcastle on the beach.

'That's me beside Michael there — I was two years younger and I hero-worshipped him. I used to follow him everywhere and he was so patient. He never let on that he minded his kid sister tagging on, but I suppose he must have done sometimes. We were always a pair, you know?' She glanced up and met Jo's eyes.

'There were other children in the family, too, weren't there?' Jo remarked.

'Oh, yes. Three other brothers, but they were quite a bit younger than us, and they more or less stuck together. People called them 'The Three Musketeers',' she said with a smile. But the smile soon faded and she paused for a moment.

'Then the war came. And Michael

got called up like all the other boys and, of course, had to go.'

'We heard a bit about you all from Walter — Walter Rogers. Do you remember him?' Jo asked.

Patricia's eyes widened.

'Walter? Oh, yes. Is he still up at Cliff Cottage?'

Jo nodded.

'Oh, I must go and see him,' Patricia said eagerly, 'I'd love a chat about the old days.'

'He'll be thrilled to bits to see you,' John remarked. 'He doesn't get many visitors.'

'I met Walter when he first bought the cottage,' Patricia said. 'Before that, it belonged to an artist who used it as a holiday retreat — I used to look after it and keep it clean for him.'

'Charles Wallace!' Jo was on the edge of her seat, her face alight with interest.

Patricia looked surprised.

'That's right — how did you know?'

'It's a long story,' Jo replied. 'I'll explain later. Can you tell me about him?'

'Oh, well now. Let me see.' Her brow furrowed in thought. 'I'll tell you something, though — I did have a strange experience up there once. One day, when I knew Mr Wallace was staying in the cottage, he didn't answer the door when I knocked, so I let myself in with my key and called out to him. I could hear his voice talking upstairs and I thought he had a visitor, but when he came down he said no, I must have been mistaken. And I've never forgotten it, because it was so strange. I know I heard him talking — as clearly as if he was in the same room, you know? Then it stopped short suddenly — almost as if he'd been switched off!'

Jo sat riveted as she listened to this story, her eyes never leaving Patricia's face, until her father spoke.

'It was Walter who told Jo how much Michael hated the idea of war and having to leave the farm and the countryside, you know?'

Patricia's face clouded.

'It was the end of childhood for us

all,' she whispered. 'Nothing would ever be the same again, you see. Because he — he just disappeared, and the not knowing what had happened to him was so awful, I thought I would never get over it.'

She sniffed and went on.

'I can remember the details still, after all this time — Michael had been home on leave and it was a dark, overcast night when he had to go back. He set off to walk into Penzance to catch the train — and we never saw him again. When we had no news for so long my parents contacted his regiment and discovered that he had never returned.' She shrugged.

'There seemed to be no other explanation but that he'd absconded, you see. But when they started calling him a coward and a deserter — I can't tell you what it did to us all . . . the shame . . . it was terrible. We had to pack up and leave our home, leave Cornwall, to get away from the pointing fingers, the whispers . . . oh, you can't imagine what it was like . . . '

Patricia reached for a handkerchief and removed her spectacles to wipe her streaming eyes.

'Do you know, there were even rumours being spread around that Michael had gone over to the Germans? Just because a couple of fishermen had spotted a U-boat in the bay, about the time he disappeared. How cruel people can be — and these were neighbours that we'd known all our lives! Oh, yes, war does some strange things to people — I pray there'll never be another one . . . '

Jo squeezed Patricia's shoulder sympathetically, and there was a pause while they gave her time to recover herself.

'I'm sorry.' Patricia blew her nose and smiled through her tears as she looked fondly at the snapshots again, her eyes lingering on her brother's face. 'Of course, I never for one moment believed that he'd deserted. Michael was the most honest man I ever knew and a stickler for duty and honour. It just wasn't in him to do such a thing.'

She leaned across to Jo.

'I can't tell you, my dear, how glad I am to know that I was right. And after all these years!'

Jo looked into her face and thought how tired the old lady was looking. All this reminiscing must be very taxing for her. She nodded and smiled.

'We'll go up to the site tomorrow and show you the quarry,' she said, glancing at the clock. 'And take you to see Walter, and anywhere else you would like to go. But it's getting quite late — I expect you'll be wanting to get to bed soon, won't you?'

'I will, my dear, it's been a long day. But it's been lovely talking to you.'

An Accident

'I'm afraid we shall have to bring Sophie with us today,' Jo said apologetically, over breakfast. 'Margaret has come down with a streaming cold and is feeling quite poorly with it. I can't expect her to look after Sophie, and I don't want her to catch it in any case. And Dad wants to come with us, of course, to see the latest progress at the dig, so there we are.' She shrugged.

'Sophie's a lovely little girl, and very well-behaved. She won't be any trouble, I'm sure,' Patricia replied. 'As a matter of fact, she reminds me of my own little granddaughter, who's slightly older than Sophie — she's eight.'

Nick was at the site when they arrived, for which Jo was glad, as it meant she could conveniently introduce Patricia to him. Then, while John took Patricia down to the quarry, Jo and Nick stayed on chatting. She was glad of the opportunity to bring him up to date on all the information she had gleaned from Bessie Phillips, as well as what Patricia had told her about Charles Wallace.

Jo had left Sophie in the office with

Kay, having thoughtfully put a colouring book and some crayons in the car before they set out, so she was able to spend some time with Nick going over all the details.

'I could just be jumping to conclusions,' Jo said finally, 'but when Patricia told us that story about the 'voice upstairs', I immediately thought of a radio transmitter. What do you reckon?'

'Could be, I suppose,' Nick replied, but he didn't sound convinced.

'But — together with the sighting of a German submarine in the bay?' Jo raised an eyebrow. 'And the fact that he was German by birth?'

Nick smiled down at her eager face.

'It makes a good case, I admit,' he said. 'But we shall have to report all this to Andy and let him decide on the final verdict.

'I'm going down in the quarry now,' he went on. 'There's something I want to look at — I thought I noticed another of those post-hole slabs sticking out. Something seems to have shifted. I may be totally wrong, but it's worth a look.'

'OK. I'm going to take Patricia over to have a chat with Walter and pick her up later,' Jo replied.

★ ★ ★

After a quick cup of tea at Walter's, Jo left the two elderly folk settling down for what was obviously going to be a long chat, and returned to the site. She had parked the car and was crossing the compound humming a little tune to herself, when she heard urgent shouts and a voice calling her name.

Turning in alarm, she could see Ryan racing towards her from the direction of the quarry.

Waving his arms and pointing back over his shoulder, he came nearer, gasping for breath as Jo ran to meet him.

'Jo — there's been an accident at the quarry — '

'An accident?' Jo's throat constricted with fear.

'It's Nick. He's had a fall. I'm going to ring for an ambulance.' He sped on towards the office while Jo, with a sinking heart and a flash of déjà vu, took to her heels and ran towards the quarry.

Below her now and in the distance, she could see a knot of people coming up the road from the quarry entrance. She could make out Graham, Lesley and some of the student volunteers. And they were carrying a body between them.

Jo's hand flew to her mouth as her stomach did a sickening somersault. Then she was pounding down the slope, and by the time she reached them they had laid their burden down on the grass. Nick's face was scratched and bruised and there was a rapidly swelling lump on his head. His eyes were closed and his skin beneath the tan was bloodless.

Jo gasped, and falling on her knees beside him put a hand on his forehead. Nick grunted, his eyes opened a crack and he made an attempt at a lop-sided grin, but winced with pain instead.

How could she put into words how worried she had been, tell Nick how much she cared about him? All her relief at finding that he was not seriously hurt vented itself in fury.

'How could you be so careless!' she ranted. 'How many times have I told you never to go down in that place without a hard hat, without a rope, without all the safety stuff we provide especially to keep you out of trouble? You're lucky you weren't killed, and if you were, you'd have no-one but yourself to blame!' Jo was blinded by tears and totally unaware of what she was saying, until she felt Lesley's hand beneath her elbow and found she was being raised to her feet.

'Hush, Jo,' the other girl said gently. 'That's enough. You need to know exactly what happened. The ambulance is here now. Come back with me and I'll tell you the full story.'

Brave Man

Back in the office, Kay, with a dazed look on her face, was cuddling Sophie on her lap while John sat beside her with an arm around them both. The little girl's shorts were torn and dirty, her knees covered in sticking plaster and her hair full of bits of vegetation.

Jo gasped as she entered and Sophie jumped down and ran towards her.

'Mummy, Mummy,' she called and Jo swung her up into her arms.

'Goodness — not more trouble!' she exclaimed. 'Whatever happened to you?'

'I went out to see if you were coming — then I saw some pretty flowers,' the little girl said. 'I wanted to pick them for you but I couldn't reach. So I climbed down the rocks a bit — and then I fell over. I cut my knee — look — and it was bleeding!' Her face puckered up and she began to cry.

Kay's face was ashen.

'Jo, I blame myself entirely,' she said.

'I just went across next door to make a cup of coffee — Sophie was sitting here good as gold with her colouring book — and when I came back she was gone! She must have got bored and slipped outside.' She ran a hand over her face.

'I ran out to look for her and the next thing I knew, there was Nick climbing out of the quarry with Sophie in his arms. He handed her up and then just sort of slipped backwards — a loose stone must have given way or something and he fell on to the same ledge where Sophie had been stuck.'

Jo listened horror-struck to the hair-raising chain of events.

'Do you mean . . . Nick was rescuing Sophie — and that was how he was hurt?'

'That's what I wanted you to know, Jo,' Lesley said gently.

Jo looked back at her with eyes like saucers as she felt all the blood drain from her face. She put Sophie down with arms that were shaking and the child ran over to perch on her grandfather's knee.

Jo clapped a hand to her mouth at the recollection of what she had said to Nick — to that brave man who had risked his own life to save her child.

7

Good News For John

Jo was beside herself with guilt. Nick had been hurt saving her daughter, and all she could do was shout at him!

Jo would have jumped into the car and headed for the hospital that minute had it not been for her other responsibilities. Her father and Sophie needed to be taken home and she had to collect Patricia as well. Also, she had a duty to their guest for the rest of the day, and it was only after Jo had seen her on to the train the next morning that she could at last turn the car up the A30 and head for Truro and the hospital.

'Mr Angove?' The receptionist glanced at her notes and ran a finger down the page. 'Are you a relative of his?' she enquired.

'No, a friend,' Jo replied, tapping a foot in impatience. The woman shook her head.

'Then I'm sorry, madam, but Mr Angove is in shock and is not allowed visitors other than his family. He has to be kept quiet for a day or two. I know his mother is with him at the moment. Can I give her a message at all to pass on to him?'

Jo shook her head. Her face fell and her heart sank like a lead weight. After all that . . . she still couldn't see him. It was too much. Jo sank into a chair in the crowded waiting-room and rubbed her hands over her face. She had no option but to return home and try again tomorrow.

★   ★   ★

As Jo entered the house she was surprised to see her father, his face wreathed in smiles, coming down the passage to meet her.

'Jo — this letter has just arrived

— it's really exciting . . . ' He thrust it under her nose as they walked together down to the kitchen. Jo cast her bag and car keys on to the table and took it from him with a frown.

'Who's it from?' she asked, scanning the text and not taking in a word of it, her mind being still on the failed trip to the hospital and her head full of Nick.

'It's there at the bottom, look!' Her father seized the letter from her impatiently and pointed a finger. 'The Chief Bard of the Cornish Gorsedd! That's who it's from!'

'Oh, yes?' Jo said, forcing herself to concentrate.

Her father gave her a puzzled look.

'You do know, I suppose, who they are,' he said with heavy sarcasm, and Jo tried to pull herself together.

'Of course I do. The society that keeps the old Cornish traditions alive. And honours people who contribute in some way to promoting Cornish subjects.'

'Yes, exactly,' John said, mollified. 'Well, they've invited me to become a member!' He glanced at the letter again.

' . . . *in recognition of a life of service to Cornish archaeology, with particular reference to the site presently under excavation.*'

Jo felt a real smile light up her face.

'That's fantastic, Dad, I'm really pleased for you.' Then she added, 'I wasn't allowed to see Nick — he has to rest for a day or two.'

'Oh, I'm sorry about that — how is he now? They haven't found anything serious, I hope?'

'Oh, no, he'll be all right,' she replied. 'It's mostly due to shock, I think. Would you like a cup of coffee?'

'No, thanks, I'm going to phone Kay and tell her my news.' As he stumped out of the room, left unspoken but hanging in the air nevertheless was the echo of her father's thoughts . . . *perhaps she'll show a bit more enthusiasm . . .*

★ ★ ★

The following day, having taken the precaution of phoning first, Jo returned to the hospital. She was delighted to find that Nick was out of bed and sitting in the day-room. Also that he was by himself. Now at last she would have the chance to say all that she needed to.

'Hi, Jo.' He smiled as she entered, but Jo thought how pale he looked.

'How are you feeling — where were you hurt — what do they say about you?' The words tumbled out in a flood and Nick smiled and held up a hand to halt the flow.

'Not bad. All over, but mostly my legs. I'll live,' he replied.

'Nick, I — I owe you a huge apology . . . ' Jo blurted out, just as a bustling nurse came in, wielding a thermometer.

'Just pop this in your mouth for me, Mr Angove,' she said, seizing his wrist and timing his pulse in the same brisk movement. She made a note on her clipboard and withdrew, but the moment was lost.

The day-room was beginning to fill up with other patients. The bursts of laughter and good-natured banter in loud male voices all around them was making it impossible to carry on with any sort of private conversation.

Someone had switched on the TV in the corner, and although nobody was watching it as it babbled inanely to itself, it was another intrusive presence. As the talk between them then turned to generalities and medical matters Jo began to despair. She could hear herself and Nick talking to each other like a couple of polite strangers, and wondered if there would ever be an opportunity to tell him all that she wanted to say.

Eventually, seeing how hopeless the position was, she gave up and said her goodbyes.

'Let me know as soon as you're home again,' she said, and left.

Jo's Chance

Two days later, unable to wait any longer, Jo contacted Nick's mother to ask after him, and to her delight, Nick came to the phone himself.

'Can you come round if you're free?' he said briefly, after they had exchanged the usual platitudes. 'I've been told to exercise these leg muscles and it's so boring tramping around on my own. We could go down to the beach for a walk.'

At last — here was the chance that she had been waiting for, to clear the air and explain. Jo was on her way in an hour.

They strolled across the dunes towards the wide expanse of Hayle beach. The tide was a long way out and the sandy crescent of the bay stretched for three miles between St Ives in one direction and Gwithian and Godrevy in the other, bisected by the tidal river which had in the past made the industrial town of Hayle into a thriving port.

'So how are your legs?' Jo asked, as they went carefully down the steps and on to the sand. 'I can see that you're limping.'

'Oh, just a bit stiff,' Nick replied with a grunt as he clutched at the handrail for support. 'They'll be all right in a day or two, but I've been told not to sit around too much.' He smiled down at her. 'Thanks for coming round, Jo. It's lovely to have some company.'

As they reached the firm and flat sands and began to stroll around the point, Jo took a deep breath.

'Nick,' she said, 'I owe you an enormous apology.' She stopped and looked him in the face. 'When you fell down the quarry — I had no idea that it had anything to do with Sophie then, you see. I jumped to a totally wrong conclusion and I yelled at you.' She swallowed hard. 'I said things that were just not true, and I was arrogant and bossy . . . and . . . '

Nick turned towards her and his eyes were gentle.

'It's OK,' he said surprisingly. 'It was only your reaction to the shock. Shock makes people behave irrationally sometimes.'

'You mean you're not mad at me?' Jo's brows rose in astonishment and she felt as if an enormous weight had suddenly rolled off her shoulders. 'I've been feeling terrible about myself ever since.'

Guilt

Nick had slipped his hands into the pockets of his jeans and with eyes cast down was idly kicking at the sand as they walked on.

'When I was laid up in hospital I had plenty of time to think, Jo. And I know that you're not really like that.'

'You do?'

Nick briefly looked up at her and there was an unreadable expression on his face.

'In fact, there are a lot of things I

need to say to you.' He paused with his hand on a flat, sun-warmed slab of rock. 'Let's sit down here for a minute. I'll make up for it by walking twice as far later on.'

He carefully lowered himself and stretched out his long legs as Jo perched beside him and leaned back into the curve of the rock. It was very quiet. Here they were away from the summer crowds, who preferred to gather with their children below the beach café around the corner. The two of them sat by rock-pools fringed with coloured weed, where small fish silently darted and where the water was clear and clean, scoured daily as it was by the restless tides.

'I've been wanting to talk to you for ages but we never seemed to be alone for long enough.'

'I know,' Jo replied. 'I had the same — '

'Jo,' he broke in, reaching for her hand although his eyes were staring far out to sea, 'you see, I owe you an apology, too.' He turned to meet her startled look.

'You do?'

He nodded.

'For things that happened long, long ago. After the accident, you know? When Dad . . . ' He squeezed her hand painfully hard. 'Jo, I realise now that I took all my own guilt and rage out on you, when you'd done absolutely nothing to deserve it.'

He looked into her face with anguish in his eyes.

'With hindsight I can see now that it was all in my subconscious mind, but it was still unforgivable of me. I know I hurt you badly, but afterwards I could never find the right words to explain to you how . . . '

Jo cupped her other hand around his.

'I understand that now as well,' she reassured him. 'But in those dreadful circumstances . . . we were only teen-agers, after all, and not experienced enough to cope with such a huge tragedy. The shock alone was enough to stop you thinking straight, goodness knows.'

Jo bit her lip and stared out at sea.

'For your father and the other fisherman both to be drowned — it seemed too awful to be true — especially over a simple thing like making a cup of tea!' There were tears in her eyes as she relived the dreadful time. 'For that gas canister to blow up! It wasn't even as if they were in dangerous waters or anything.' She brushed a hand across her eyes.

Nick shook his head and scuffed a foot in the sand, avoiding Jo's gaze.

'When was life ever fair?' He shrugged. 'The worst thing for me was the guilt,' he said quietly.

Jo looked at him in astonishment.

'Why should you have felt guilty, for goodness' sake?'

Nick ran a hand through his hair which was already dishevelled by the sea breezes.

'Because Dad had asked me to go

along on the trip with them, but I'd already promised to take you rambling and climbing around Carn Galver that weekend with Rachel and Paul, so I couldn't. And Jo, when I heard what had happened I felt that if I'd only been there, I might have been able to save them.'

'Oh, Nick, that's ridiculous!' Jo said gently. 'If you had been there, you would just as likely have been thrown out of the boat, too.'

'I know. But if we hadn't been staying down west in that remote spot, out of touch with the outside world, I would at least have been there for Mother and the rest of them when it happened. Instead, it was the next day before I even knew about it at all.'

'There was nothing you could have done,' Jo said, squeezing his hand. 'Don't be so hard on yourself. It was more than ten years ago — it's time to move on. You can't torture yourself for ever.'

'I Still Love You'

They fell into silence, remembering those sad days.

'Then I went away to college,' Jo said softly, 'and we drifted apart.'

Nick nodded.

'And I abandoned my hopes of a career to look after Mum and the others.' As their eyes met, he spoke quietly. 'But, Jo, my feelings for you never changed over the years. I loved you then and I still love you, but the longer time went on the more I realised what a fool I'd been not to admit it. And since we've been together these last months I've been trying to find a way to tell you that.'

He gazed out to sea again.

'But I can't expect you to feel the same — you've come a long way since then. You have a full life, lots of commitments and another . . . close friend now.' He shrugged. 'So there we are,' he finished, with a smile which didn't reach his eyes. 'I just wanted you to know.'

Jo listened in amazement to his story. Nick loved her! And always had done! She could hardly believe it.

'Oh, Nick, I had no idea . . . ' she whispered and gripped his arm as she turned her face up to him. 'I've never loved anyone else but you, either. But you see, when I went away to college — it was only two months after the tragedy, and all that was still hanging over me. I couldn't forget it, or you. And I thought you blamed me for it, and would never want to see me again.' She covered her face with her hands.

'I eventually married Mark mainly because I felt so alone and so vulnerable. It was the worst reason for getting married, I know that now. We were like chalk and cheese and it was bound to be a disaster.' Jo's shoulders hunched as she clasped both arms around her knees and rested her chin on them.

'The only good thing to come out of it all was Sophie.'

And that's the way it'll stay, I

suppose, she was thinking sadly. Even if Nick was considering a long-term relationship between them, it was too much to expect of him — to take on another man's child.

Then something Nick had said suddenly registered and she glanced up at him with a frown.

'Nick, what was that you said about me having a 'close friend'? Who were you talking about?'

'Well, your boyfriend from London, of course. Russell, is he called? The big archaeologist chap.'

'Russell?' Jo's eyes widened in amazement, and she almost burst out laughing. 'He's not my boyfriend — well, not in the way you mean — he's just a friend.'

Nick scowled at her.

'So all those hugs and kisses meant nothing at all, is that what you're trying to say?'

He's jealous, Jo thought, dizzy with happiness, and laid a hand over his.

'That's just Russell's nature, Nick.

He's like that with everyone — expansive, demonstrative — he's that kind of person. We were at college together and I know him well. But that's all. OK?'

Nick put both arms around her and buried his face in her hair, as Jo found herself both laughing and crying.

They stayed where they were in their secluded nook for some time, with only the seabirds and the sound of the waves for company, saying all that was in their hearts until no vestige of the past was left to come between them ever again. Neither of them mentioned the future.

Positive Identification

'I'll take you back to see Dad, if you like,' Jo said as they returned to normal life and walked back from the beach. 'He hasn't seen you for ages and until you can drive again you won't be going far, will you?'

'Great idea, thanks.' Nick eased his stiff legs into the car. 'I would be glad of a change of scenery. Mum's been fussing over me so much lately that it's getting a bit claustrophobic at home.' He grinned and raised an eyebrow. 'She means well, but I'm not exactly helpless, as I try to tell her.'

They arrived back to find that John must already have a visitor, as a strange car was parked in the drive. John came out to meet them in the hall.

'Hello, you two. Good to see you, Nick. How are you?' The two men shook hands and they covered the topic of the accident and its consequences.

'Andy's just arrived to tell us all the latest about the case,' John went on.

'I'm glad you're here,' the inspector said with a smile. 'Saves me having to say everything twice. I was just congratulating John on his exciting news. Recognition by the Old Cornwall Society, no less!'

'That's fantastic news, John. Well done!' Nick said sincerely as he clapped him on the back.

They had all found somewhere to sit

and there was some more banter as Nick settled himself beside John and they both supported their injured limbs on a shared footstool. Then after the initial chit-chat was over, Andy came to the purpose of his call and took out his notes.

'We've been following several leads over Charles Wallace, and that information you two gave us was really useful.' He turned to Nick and Jo, who were sitting close beside each other on the settee. 'I've had contacts in London going through the records, and they have verified that he was originally of German nationality, but became a British citizen and changed his name when he became a public figure.'

He pulled out his spectacles and checked the documents on his knee.

'Then the pathologists reported finding traces of paint under the fingernails of the second skeleton.' He looked over the top of the lenses and raised an eyebrow.

'Really?' Jo's face lit up with interest.

'Oh, yes.' He followed the text with a finger. 'And the fabric fibres turned out to be fragments of leather — presumably from a jacket.'

'Or elbow patches!' Jo exclaimed, straightening suddenly in her seat. 'Bessie — that's Mrs Philips — said that Charles Wallace always wore an old sweater with leather patches on the elbows.'

'Is that so?' The inspector's eyes widened. 'Hmm. So it all seems to fit the picture we have of Charles Wallace. Although we still have a report to come back of the dental records, I think we can safely say that he's our man. Which means that the second skeleton has now been positively identified.'

'Brilliant,' Nick said. 'Do we have any idea why he and Michael Laity should have had a fight up by the quarry on that night?'

Andy Farr took a deep breath and lost himself in thought for a moment.

'We're as near certain as we can get, given the evidence that we have,' he

217

said eventually. 'Call it a ninety-nine per cent hunch.' He consulted his notes again. 'We think that Charles Wallace was indeed spying for the Germans.'

There was total silence in the room.

'The reasons for coming to this conclusion are, one — the signalling lamp that was found near him in the quarry. Two — the fact that he worked for the coastguard department and would have access to shipping movements. Three — that a German sub was known to have been in the area at that time, and four — the mysterious voice that Michael's sister heard, which I'm pretty convinced was coming from a hidden radio transmitter.' He looked gravely round at them all. 'So there we are.'

'That does seem pretty conclusive,' John said thoughtfully. 'And if Michael Laity had come across him that night using the lantern — '

' — to signal to the waiting submarine — ' Jo eagerly broke in.

' — he would have challenged

him — ' Nick added.

' — and they had a fight and fell over the edge,' John finished.

A silence fell as they all pictured the tragic scene. Andy was the first to rouse himself.

'Yes,' he said slowly and replaced his papers in their folder. 'I think we can safely say that the case is now closed.'

Unsung Hero

'So the police have closed the file on the case.'

John and Jo were holding a team meeting at the site to bring everyone up to date with all that had been happening. Crowded into the Portak-abin which was the office and general workroom, each person was perched where there was a space to be found, all listening with interest as John filled them in on the last pieces of the jigsaw.

'Wow!' Graham gave a low whistle. 'So, far from being a coward and a deserter, Michael Laity was an unsung hero. And no-one would have known any different if it hadn't been for us!'

'I almost feel as if I know him,' Jo said softly. 'He's become such a part of our lives in these last few months.'

'One thing that occurred to me, though,' Nick said, 'was why nobody seems to have missed Charles Wallace after he disappeared. You'd think, even if he had no family, that people from his work would have come over here looking for him.'

'Oh!' Jo replied. 'Patricia did mention that actually, when I was taking her back to the station. Apparently he was in a lot of debt. He owed huge amounts all over the place and when he vanished, everyone assumed that he was running from his creditors.'

There were nods of understanding round the room.

'Then,' she went on, 'when he couldn't be traced, they thought that he must have done a bunk and left the country. And as it was wartime, communications abroad were so difficult that the search for him was eventually abandoned.'

'It's a sad story,' Lesley said. 'I think there ought to be some sort of public recognition of Michael Laity to clear his name, don't you?'

'Yes. Patricia did suggest that,' John agreed. 'I'm going to see what can be arranged.' He cleared his throat and paused for a moment. 'And now to other business.' He looked around the room.

'There are several reasons why I've called you all together today. Chiefly because I've had some big news from Russell. Thanks to his enthusiasm and drive, English Heritage have agreed to take over all the preservation and administration of the site.' He beamed and spread his hands expansively. 'They'll sponsor any more work that needs to be done, then eventually open it to the public.'

There was a sudden round of applause at this, then Ryan shifted his large frame which was wedged into a shaky folding chair and leaned forward, his eyes alight with excitement.

Honour

'Brilliant!' he exclaimed. 'You know, this has been quite something for me, to have been involved in such a big and important project on my first real job. It'll look good on the CV, that's for sure!'

'Same here,' Lesley said with a grin.

'Well, I would like to say a big 'thank you' to you all,' John said, 'and especially to Jo, who took over so efficiently with no preparation, at a minute's notice.'

There was another small burst of applause and Jo rose to her feet to speak.

'Thank you, too,' she said simply. 'I've really enjoyed working with you all.' She glanced towards her father and went on.

'And there's something else that you should know, but Dad's too modest to tell you himself.' She grinned at her father and noticed to her amusement that he was actually blushing as she announced the honour that he had received from the Old Cornwall Society, and this time the applause was loud and long.

When it had died away, Jo noticed with some surprise that her father was struggling to his feet and holding up a hand for silence again. Wondering what was coming next, she watched as his already flushed face turned a deeper shade, then realised with amazement that he was actually looking self-conscious.

'Before you go, there is one more announcement I want to make,' he said, and a beaming smile spread across his face. 'A personal one. I would like you to know that Kay has consented to be my wife. We are planning to be married in the autumn — and you're all invited to the wedding!'

He sat down to such a chorus of

congratulations and applause that the tiny building was shaking as Jo came forward to give them both a hug and her own sincere good wishes for a happy future together.

Everlasting Peace

John put the phone down just as Jo entered the house. 'That was Andy,' he said. 'Now that the case is closed, the police have released the bones of the two men for burial. There's to be a joint funeral for them at Penzance as soon as it can be arranged. I must let Patricia know right away.'

'Yes, of course. I expect she'll bring as many of the family with her as are able to come,' Jo replied. 'That'll be good.' She paused for a moment. 'But what about Charles Wallace — did they ever trace any relatives of his?'

Her father shook his head.

'No, the police even had Interpol on

to it, searching through their records, but nothing came up.'

'It's a bit sad really, to think that he'll have no-one of his own there,' Jo added pensively, 'even though he was a traitor. But we'll all go, of course — and I expect Walter will as well. And Patricia knew him, too — she'll be able to represent both men, in a way.'

'Perhaps someone from the art world — or Wallace's publishing firm — might turn up if we contact them,' John added, warming to the theme. 'That'll be enough to ensure that he's not completely overlooked.'

'Good idea,' Jo said. 'And I hear there's to be a special service for Michael on another occasion, too, when a public vindication of his name will be made. Is that right?'

John nodded.

'Yes, and that's not all. It's going to be added to the war memorial as well, along with all those from the district who fell in battle.'

'I'm really pleased about that,' Jo said

quietly. 'It'll mean so much to Patricia, won't it?'

★ ★ ★

When the day of the funeral came round, the church was impressively full for the simple but dignified ceremony as the two men were laid to rest. Whatever their different backgrounds had been, and the differences of the two opposing sides which they had taken when the world was in chaos, they were united now in death.

'Everything passes,' the minister intoned, and these two had found everlasting peace at last — together.

A few days later, the same crowd gathered at the war memorial in the village square, which now proudly bore the name of Michael Laity upon its granite cross. Members of the British Legion led the procession of local dignitaries, friends and family to their positions around it and the chairman of the council then made a moving speech.

As the local band was playing 'Abide With Me', Jo looked about her at the people she knew, and a great many whom she did not, who had all come to pay their respects to a brave and misjudged young man. And she fervently hoped that this recognition, late though it was, had in a small way helped to make up to the Laity family for the pain which they had suffered during those dreadful wartime years.

Then, when it was all over, Patricia, with tears streaming down her face, came forward and squeezed Jo's hand.

'Thank you, my dear, oh, thank you so much. I can't tell you what this has meant to me, and to the rest of us. Bless you all — I shall never forget this day as long as I live.'

'We Need To Talk'

'I'll drop you back home,' Jo said to Nick after the ceremony. 'Then I must go back to the site and get some work done. There are some loose ends to be tied up and I seem to have been slacking a lot lately — what with one thing and another!' She smiled up as she turned the key in the ignition and headed out on to the main road.

'That was a very good ceremony, wasn't it?' Nick said reflectively. 'I was quite impressed.'

'I was a bit overcome myself at the end,' Jo admitted. 'I found it very touching, but it was a lovely way to round off the whole business.'

'Talking of rounding things off — it's great news about your father and Kay, isn't it?' Nick said, stretching out his legs as far as the confines of his seat would allow.

'Oh, yes.' Jo's face softened. 'I'm so pleased for them. Dad's been on his own for such a long time.'

'But where will this leave you?' Nick enquired, voicing what Jo had left unsaid, even to herself.

'Now that the dig is coming to an end as well,' Nick went on, 'what plans do you have for yourself and Sophie? Will you carry on living where you are after the wedding?'

'I don't know, Nick,' Jo said in a small, strained voice. 'I don't see how I can.'

'Pull into this next lay-by for a minute — we need to talk,' he said tersely.

Jo, with a quick sideways glance at him, pulled up by the estuary of the Hayle river where flocks of seabirds were foraging along the tideline. She pulled on the handbrake and silence fell for a moment as Nick reached for her hand.

'Jo, you know how much I love you, don't you?' he said. 'Would you — could you consider a future which included us both together?'

Jo's heart lurched. There was nothing she could possibly want more — but . . . it was not going to be that simple. She kept her eyes on a couple of brilliantly white egrets that were stalking along the shoreline together.

'Oh, Nick, I love you, too. But aren't you forgetting something — someone?' She gently withdrew her hand. 'I've got a child, a small child, who will be my responsibility for many years to come. I'm not free to share your life, you see.'

She turned away and looked unseeingly out of the window to hide the tears which threatened to spill over at any moment.

But Nick placed both hands on her shaking shoulders and was turning her back to face him.

'Jo, you fool, why on earth should Sophie be a problem? She's a great little kid — I like her and I think she likes me. And I'd like to help you to bring her up, if you'll let me.'

Then Jo's tears changed to tears of joy and she grasped Nick's hands, laughing. There was no doubt in her mind now as to where her future lay.

TWISTED TAPESTRIES

Joyce Johnson

Jenna Pascoe is a Cornish fisherman's daughter. When her parents receive news that her mother's sister, aunt Olive, is coming home to England from Italy, they refuse to acknowledge her. Family secrets resurface and Jenna's initial delight turns to dismay. However, Olive and her family turn up at their home, and Jenna meets her handsome cousin Allesandro. How will the families resolve their differences — and how will cousins, Jenna and Allesandro cope with their growing feelings for each other . . . ?

A STRANGER'S LOVE

Valerie Holmes

Megan has good reason to hate the prosperous Ackton family, the mill owners whom she holds responsible for her mother's death. However, determined that they will not shorten her life, she runs away. After falling into a canal, she is accused of being a madwoman for attempting suicide, and is sent to the asylum. Megan is rescued from her fate by Mr Nathan Ackton, and finds that she owes her liberty to a member of the family she loathes.

COME, CATHERINE

Nina Louise Moore

When Catherine visits the Constantines at Treworgey, her stay is longer than she anticipated. She becomes involved in the lives of Aunt Ada, Mimsy and Uncle Lando, and doesn't want to leave. She agrees to a 'marriage of convenience' to the head of the family, Edward, intending to earn her place in the household. But when Paula Penlove returns to the neighbouring estate, she realizes that she loves her 'husband' — but is it too late to tell him so . . . ?